THE AUTHOR

Dorothy Hamilton has lived in Delaware County, Indiana, all her life. She attended school at Cowan, Muncie Central High, and Ball State University. She has been active in professional writing courses, first as a student and later as an instructor.

Mrs. Hamilton grew up in the Methodist Church and devoted much of her life to rearing seven children.

Then she felt led to become a private tutor. Several hundred girls and boys have come to Mrs. Hamilton for gentle encouragement, for renewal of their self-esteem, and to improve their schoolwork.

Since 1967 she has had fifty serials, more than fifty short stories, and several articles published in religious magazines. She has also written for radio and newspaper.

Mrs. Hamilton is author of a growing shelf of books: **Anita's Choice, Christmas for Holly, Charco, The Killdeer, Tony Savala, Jim Musco, Settled Furrows, Kerry, The Blue Caboose, Mindy, The Quail, The Gift of a Home, Jason,** and **Busboys at Big Bend.**

THE EAGLE

Dorothy Hamilton

HERALD PRESS
Scottdale, Pennsylvania
Kitchener, Ontario
1974

Library of Congress Cataloging in Publication Data

Hamilton, Dorothy, 1906-
  The Eagle.

  I. Title.
PZ4.H218Eag [PS3558.A425]   813'.5'4   74-13069
ISBN 0-8361-1748-4

To David Hamilton,
the history teacher in my family.

The Patriarch

By Frederick M. Hinshaw

Far above birds of field and copse,
   the sparrow hawk and the redtail,
   is domain of the bald eagle — without fail
his surveillance never stops.

Not like the golden eagle of the West
   his range is coast to coast — along land
   and water — always close at hand
is this bird's tall tree for perch and nest.

The old man reminds me of that bird
   of legend — sharp-eyed and white crowned —
   seldom from his eminence coming down
to the realm of lesser ones to be heard.

Most of all his lofty dignity —
   all-seeing and to some all-wise,
   the vision in those aging eyes —
still sharp enough for him to see.

1

Matthew Kirk was perched on a vantage point from which he could overlook the town of Oak Hill where he'd lived for forty-one of his seventy years. He pulled the high back rocker to the southeast corner of the wide porch he'd built on the side of the garage. He shoved the chair into motion with one heel and thought as he'd done many times before, *Folks would be a lot better off if twine chair seats were in style. They allow for settling in.*

Then he smiled at himself. *Maybe it's a good thing all my unusual ideas didn't catch on. Otherwise this town wouldn't be the same. And I don't know as I'd like that.*

Certainly no one had followed the example of building a veranda on the side of a garage. And it had taken Matthew some time to nullify Nancy's objections which began with, "Where in the world did you ever get an idea like that?"

"In a way you're responsible," Matthew said. "You were the one who insisted we go over beyond Bundy Avenue one day when we were in New Castle. To that fruit stand.

"I surveyed the surroundings while I waited for you

7

to pick out three pounds of tomatoes," Matthew continued. "No use to stare at a dashboard when there's something different to be seen. I looked across a vacant lot and saw a small brown house. Couldn't have been more than four rooms in it. Out back was a garage with a porch. Right away I could see how useful it would be. For family gatherings, a play place for children. I could see myself potting plants and you stringing beans. That's all I got accomplished. You came back to the car."

"But we already have room for all of this," Nancy said. "In the basement, the side porch, and the house. You know I never object to having any kind of family activity."

"I know that for a fact," Matt said. "Up to now that is. I figure there are a few things you'd not allow. Such as — well, none comes to mind right at this minute. The point is, are you saying no?"

"Matthew Kirk, have I ever objected to anything you really and seriously wanted to do? That's not counting the things you never meant to do in the first place, like going up in a balloon and raising crickets to sell to fishermen and starting a museum in Oak Hill."

"You're wrong on one count," Matthew said. "That last one. Maybe this town's not big enough to support or appreciate a collection of historical relics. But it's growing and that time is coming. And I'd like to be the one to get it going."

"So you're serious about the museum, are you?"

"I am. I've pondered the matter for a long time."

"Then you'll do it," Nancy said. "I don't know when or how — or *where*. Perhaps I should begin to worry

8

about that. Will I be living in the Oak Hill Museum? Will I be one of your relics?"

"No, Nancy. You'll never be of interest to me or anyone else as an antique. It's your spirit, your timelessness that's a source of wonder and pleasure to me."

"Well, thank you, sir," Nancy said. She stopped the sweeper and smoothed the strands of hair that crossed the pinkish top of his head.

Matthew recalled that conversation as he pushed the cane-seated rocker into motion. Sometimes he thought that memories were like the records he and Nancy and the grandchildren played on the mahogany phonograph. They were stored away in the cabinet of his mind to be replayed. *Some folks say their memories are failing,* Matt thought as he sniffed the May air. A person needed to take in all the fragrance of spring he could so it would be fresh in his mind through the months when the slanted sunrays bound Indiana in freezing cold. *I prefer to think we keep adding to our collection. It takes a while to sort through them.*

As Matt rocked he recalled what he'd thought after Nancy left the room the day he'd broached the subject of the porch. This recollection was clear in his mind, the grooves deep and distinct. *That was the day I came to the point of being at peace with myself about having two wives — not at the same time of course.* Even in his thoughts Matthew strove for clarity.

He'd often faced the fact that he might have an uncomfortable feeling if he and Dora and Nancy ran into each other in the hereafter. He knew what the Bible said, that in heaven men and women weren't given in marriage. That Scripture had given him considerable doubt when he was a younger man. He wasn't so sure that he anticipated such a bland existence. He wasn't that spiritual. Now and then when his daughter Susan was going through her ordeal as the wife of Dirk Garland he wondered if this wasn't part of her trouble. Maybe she was too transcendental, like Emerson and some other Concord men of letters, to fit in with the earthly — or was it earthy — nature of Bertha Garland's son.

As he thought of Nancy and Dora at the same time it came to him that they'd probably enjoy each other's company. That when the male and female labels were removed folks might find a real unity in community, either in heaven or on earth.

Matthew focused his thoughts on what he was seeing, turned the camera of his mind on the visible world. He couldn't see as much from any other spot on the premises. The lot on which he and Nancy had built their five-room brick house was on the north side of Maple Street. It sloped upward at the back to a ridge which ran parallel to the Norfolk and Western railroad tracks two blocks away. Matt wondered why the glacier which had smoothed the terrain as it inched down from the north had left such humps. He could see that the edge might have been serrated, accounting for the hills of Henry County. But what made this roll or fold in the land?

The porch extended to the south edge of this rise. That's why Matthew put the two steps at the end. They could use the flagstone stairs that led from the backyard. No need to build, and mow around, two sets.

To the east he could see the state highway which

10

connected the street which ran through the middle of Muncie to the west edge of New Castle and ran farther north and south from both towns. A cluster of new homes lay between the concrete road and the edge of Oak Hill. New ones were being constructed. That's why the lumberyard was expanding and why Matthew could work whenever he chose, except days like today.

This was Memorial Day. Oak Hill was at a semi-standstill. The grocery was open until noon, and people could pick up mail from boxes in the lobby of the post office, but not buy stamps or money orders and the carrier wouldn't run his rural route. Traffic was sparse compared to usual weekdays. No trucks roared and snorted up the gradual incline from State Road 3. Only three cars were parked beyond the white stakes at the side of the Oak Hill school building.

More bicycles than cars this morning, Matthew thought. *I wouldn't be surprised to see Little Matt come pedaling up the street.* Then he checked his thoughts. *I've got to get out of the habit of hooking that word "little" onto the boy's name. He's ten now.*

He pulled the gold watch out of his vest pocked and clicked the lid. *Nine forty-five. No hurry about setting up the picnic table. Dirk and his father won't be in from the farm for another hour or more.*

He had an impulse to walk down to the corner, and then west a block to the root beer stand. It had been open for nearly a month and he hadn't given them a dime's worth of business. *Nancy's at the store or someplace in between here and there and wouldn't be too surprised or alarmed if she discovered I deserted my post for a while.*

He stood up, still erect, buttoned his vest, pulled his gray coat sweater down so the front and back were even, and walked around to the cinder alley — the alley where feet and tires had pressed slag from countless coal fires into a gritty mosaic. Every walk Matthew Kirk took was an advanture. He never moved without noticing his surroundings. Even alleys were revelations. He knew who threw away their money by what they put in their trash bins. He could have told, if he had that kind of soul, who was too lazy or ignorant to put a new plug on the end of a light cord or to solder a handle onto an otherwise perfect tea-kettle. He knew almost without looking whose early garden would be free of bindweed, lamb's-quarters, and butter print. It was no easy job for people on the fringe of town to keep their gardens free of weeds. Seeds from adjoining fields came with every breeze.

As Matt turned on Walnut Street he thought again of the wisdom of locating the stand between the school and the main street. *They'll catch a lot of the trade that always has gone to the drugstore down on Maple.*

He recalled the first time he'd tasted root beer not too many years before. His reluctance to sample the foaming drink puzzled him. He considered himself an open-minded man. He decided that the name had set his mind against the product. He'd had plenty of opportunity to observe the waste and the damage caused by a growing appetite for alcoholic beverages. Hearing his grandchildren ask for root *beer* made him flinch.

It was Little Matt who led him to overcome this prejudice against the herb-flavored drink. They'd been out to the farm that day. Matt hadn't started to school yet and they'd driven to Springvale to get pumpkins for the little boy to sell at his stand at the end of the front walk. Matthew was in favor of this idea. He'd worried when Dirk got his inheritance. He hadn't wanted a surplus of money to spoil his grandchildren. But that hadn't happened, thanks to Susan and Dirk. They were careful not to deprive the children of the satisfaction of earning.

Frost had come late that year and the pumpkins were fully ripe, a deep orange. "They'll make fine jack-o'-lanterns," Little Matt said as he bounced up and down on the seat. "Do you think lots of kids will buy them, Grandfather?"

"What price you thinking of asking?"

"Mama said fifteen cents."

"At that price I don't think you'll have any trouble getting rid of all of them."

"I don't want to sell them all," Matt said. "I want one for me. And for Ellen if she's not too big like Neal and Mary Anne are already."

As they crossed State Road 3 Matthew Kirk said, "I'd better stop and get some gas. Want something to eat and drink?"

"Well," Matt said. "I am pretty thirsty and a little hungry."

"What do you want?" Matthew asked as they pulled up alongside the red pumps.

"I think I'll get root beer," the boy said. "Do you want some too?"

"No. I don't think I'd like it."

"Grandfather," Matt said. "You ought to try it. Then you'll get used to it and *know* if you like it or not."

13

I'll have to tell Susan about this, Matthew thought. *Tell her that her training was echoed in Little Matt's words.*

A wave of sadness shadowed Matthew's mind. The little boy who'd taught him to get used to root beer was older now, ten. He was probably too big for jack-o'-lanterns. At least he'd never be the wondering and enchanting age of five again.

Matthew shook his head as if to clear it of the cobwebs of melancholy. *That's "old" thinking. I don't have time for that. And neither do I want to give it space in my mind.*

As he waited his turn at the open window of the root beer stand he smiled. *Besides, children and childhood still are. They didn't come into existence with Little Matt or end when he grew out of the wide-eyed stage.*

He paid for his large-sized root beer and started home. He could drink as he walked. He wouldn't have been at all surprised to see Neal on a porch or walking from door to door. This was the day he collected from his paper route customers. *He could've put it off. A lot of folks will be gone because of the holiday.*

The thought of Neal stayed in his mind until he reached the alley behind the house. He felt easy in his mind about the quiet sensitive grandson. *Dirk seems to have done a fairly good job of rectifying there — as well as in his relations with Susan. I see the boy and his dad talking every now and then.*

Warmth flooded Matthew's consciousness as he thought of Susan. It was always so. *I reckon she's always represented joy to me even during the years when I saw pain in her eyes.*

He shook his head as he stopped at the back corner of the garage and dropped the empty root beer cup into the trash burner. *I mustn't give room to such thoughts. They cloud the cordial feelings I sometimes have toward Dirk. And he doesn't deserve any of my mental punishment. He's giving himself enough of that.*

He unfastened the top button of his vest as he walked up on the veranda. The sun had melted the cool of the morning into nothingness. As Matthew sat down in the rocker he thought, *This is a day of reunion, not a time of recrimination.*

2

From the headland of the age of seventy it seemed to Matthew that he'd spent most of the first fourteen years of his life hiding from people. He understood now why he'd searched for and found four separate shelters. One was in the tall walnut wardrobe in the spare bedroom. He could instantly tune in on memory's waves and be huddled in the corner, surrounded by the folds of his mother's dresses. He could only stay in this retreat for short periods of time. In summer, lack of air forced him to poke his head out of the doors or move to another hiding place. In all seasons he soon had to seek relief from the stinging scent of mothballs.

Matthew preferred the solitude of the cellar over the clothes closet. But often the way of escape to this lower level was blocked. He could never tell when his mother might sashay through the swinging doors to get lemonade for the company or to hunt a recipe for Aunt Lola. He often wondered what his aunt did with all those recipes since she ate more meals at the Kirks than she did at home.

There was another reason why Matthew didn't often hide in the cellar. Although he loved the musty smell of the cool earth he couldn't help wondering if a mouse might be scurrying down the moldy walls of stone. And every sound startled him. Bats could have flown in the ground level windows. And he'd seen a salamander once when he followed his father down the wooden stairs. He never forgot that day, not only because of the squirming scaly lizard but also because of what he learned about his father. He never went to the basement for any reason after that without darting a glance at the heavy beam that ran along the ceiling. Sometimes he thought he could see the glint of a glass bottle. He was either never sure or didn't want to be.

In all seasons except winter Matthew ran either to the Wolf River apple tree in the orchard or the corn-crib at the north end of the barn when his mother called him to play with cousins or show his aunts how his fingering on the piano keys had improved. She told anyone who stopped by, "Matthew's doing so well. He can even play "Robin's Return" now. And you know how many trilling runs there are in it."

A way to escape was not always open and he'd twist the piano stool down, open the sheet of music, and perform, considering these ordeals as one of the penalties of his life. But he never felt that he deserved such punishment. He wasn't the one who asked people to come to the house every Sunday and almost every day of the week. And as he played bar after bar until he came to the double line at the end he always thought, *If I ever have any kids I'll* never never *make them take lessons. Especially after I find out they hate it.*

Even as early as the age of eight Matthew began to understand why he needed so many hiding places. It wasn't that he didn't like any of the children in his neighborhood or at school. He and Garry C. could fill hours with fun and neither get tired of one another nor quarrel for very long at a time. *But Mama never has Garry C.'s folks over to eat,* he often thought. She *doesn't like his mother much. I don't see why. She makes kids feel good. I don't think we ever make* her *nervous.*

In fact Matthew didn't begin to think of running from whoever his mother invited until he found out who was coming or how many. Sometimes he wondered why none of the aunts or few of the people who were his mother's church friends had children his age. Some Sundays he was expected to shepherd a bunch of little kids, keep them out of mud puddles, push them — but not too hard — in the rope swing, and not let them get rough with Taffy, the collie. Matthew understood how the dog felt. So much company made *him* cross. It was just as bad when the children of guests were older. He was told to show them the stereoptican cards or play the Victrola. He was old enough to know that no one wanted to see pictures of the Eiffel Tower or the St. Louis World's Fair. And neither did they pay any attention to Harry Lauder or the singer his mother called the Great Caruso. Matthew found that it was easy to slip away from the older group. They didn't want him around any more than he wanted to be with them. After he'd climbed to the thick limb of the apple tree or ducked into the corncrib he often thought, *They probably don't even know I'm not there. I'll bet they're going right on with their whispering and giggling.*

18

The view from the apple tree perch was limited. He couldn't see far in any direction, except down. But he liked the way sunlight sifted through the trembling leaves and made moving patterns on his arms and shepherd's check knickers. And in spring when the tree was in bloom he sat in sort of a secret place of beauty and fragrance.

The slatted corncrib on the end of the barn offered more amusement than the other three retreats. He could climb to the top of the shifting heap of ears and look south through the triangular air vent. He could see Cabin Creek winding through the fields like a silver ribbon which the wind was rippling. He could see cars go into and leave the barn-like covered bridge and, if the day was still, he could hear the rumble of loose boards under the weight of moving wheels.

He liked to climb down and play butcher shop at the wooden chopping block. He picked fat ears and sliced them with the long corn knife. His arms weren't long enough so that he could grasp the razor-sharp tool by its corncob handle. He had to position the edge on the ear and hit it with the flat stone he kept hidden on a ledge by the door. He often wondered if his father ever noticed the nicks on the dull edge. But even as early as eight Matthew realized that there were times when his father didn't seem to be aware of much that went on around him. Not even of all the people who were guests in his home which was actually the house his wife had inherited. In a way the son envied the father. He didn't need to hunt hiding places. Or was he always in one? In a place about which Matthew did not know?

If no echoes of his mother's voice came from the direction of the house or yard Matthew amused himself in other ways. He carefully picked one row of grains from an ear of corn. Then he picked every other one from the next lengthwise row, alternating the pattern on the next — and the next — and the next. He liked the feeling of making a design. Sometimes he tried building a house in the same manner that his grandfather told him pioneers constructed homes of logs. But ears of corn were tapered and his houses of yellow grain sagged and fell apart.

There were a few times when Matthew went to sleep on the dirt floor of the crib. He curled up with his head on the crook of an arm and looked through the slats. He never thought that he was looking at a wall of boards. He saw only the shafts of light.

Matthew was nearly nine the time his father found him asleep in the crib of corn. This was on the day when his mother, Letitia Spencer Kirk, invited her relatives from Fort Wayne to come for the day. She was talking to Aunt Lola when Matthew heard the news that the big city branch of the Spencer family was coming. "I'm not so sure this is a good idea, Tish," Lola Allen said. "By the time they catch the interurban and ride all the way down here and you meet them in town it'll be nearly noon. And the last car goes north at four."

"This is true. But I must not neglect my obligations to Papa's side of the family."

"Fiddle-faddle," Lola said. "What obligations? They never have you up there. Nor me, for that matter."

Matthew was sitting on the second step from the bottom of the stairway which led upward from the hall which ran from the front door to the kitchen. He could hear every word of the conversation and he also added some thoughts of his own. *No wonder no one ever asks us to eat at their house. Mama has someone here all the time.*

"Will Andrew be on hand?" Aunt Lola asked. *"This* time?"

Matthew thought for a while that his mother hadn't heard the question. Then her words came out like a string of firecrackers after one end was lit. "Lola, do you have to keep needling me? You know how it is here. You know where Andrew goes and what he does. And why."

"I'm not so sure about the why," Lola said. "Oh, I know what you say in that aggrieved tone of voice. But remember this, Tish. I've known Andrew Kirk as long as you have. And I remember how he used to be."

Are they going to have a fight? Matthew wondered. He decided he'd rather not know and slipped down the hall and out the back door. He noticed that his aunt didn't come over for the next three days but she showed up on Sunday with eleven other relatives. Letitia Kirk had room for fourteen people when she put all four boards in the round dining room table and extended it to an oblong. In some way Matthew never understood why she always managed to have that many guests, no more, no less.

Only three cousins came with the delegation from Allen County. His mother said, "Matthew, you remember your cousins. You met them four or was it five years ago?" But he didn't remember. If he'd ever seen them before they didn't look like anyone he knew. *Besides, I was only four then and that littlest kid probably wasn't even born.* But he didn't say anything. His mother didn't listen to him much of the time and never when grown-ups were around.

It began to rain after they'd eaten. Matthew felt the misty drizzle on his arms as he stepped out the front door. So he headed straight for the corncrib and was there until he opened his eyes and saw his father in the doorway.

"Is it real late?" Matthew asked as he tried to shrug the numbness out of his elbow.

"Not very," his father said. "About three fifteen."

"Oh," Matthew said. He was thinking, *Papa never comes home this early. Not before dark. And mostly I don't even know when he gets here.*

"I didn't hear you drive in."

"I didn't," Andrew Kirk said. "I came up the old road. To avoid notice. I got worried about Lady."

"Cause she's going to have her colt?"

"Right you are. And so's she. I thought I'd slip her a nubbin or two before I head back."

Matthew almost asked, "Head back where?" But he couldn't get the words out all the way. No one else ever talked about where his father went when he wasn't working on the farm. At least not in front of him.

"What are you doing out here?" Andrew Kirk asked as he stooped and picked up four ears of grain.

"Hiding."

That moment of that afternoon was printed indelibly in Matthew's mind. He never forgot how he felt, nor how things looked, nor what his father said. For the first time the man and the boy who'd lived in the same house for nearly nine years had a real conversation.

Andrew Kirk sat down on the chopping block, clasped one knee in his strong brown hands, and said, "Hiding from the leeches?"

"Leeches?"

"Well, I guess that's a pretty strong word for your mother's relatives. You know what leeches are?"

"Yes, sir. They're like worms. One got on my leg once when I went swimming in the creek with Garry C. They hurt."

"They sure do. This is off the subject, Matt. But do you have to call me *sir?*"

"Well, Mama says — "

"I know. Like I'm not supposed to nickname you."

"I like it when someone does. Garry C. always calls me Matt."

"That's the boy in the tenant house on Spencer Farm, No. 2. You like him?"

"Yes. Yes. He's a lot of fun."

"Good. I have to go down there tomorrow. Want to go along?"

"I'll have to ask."

"I suppose you will. Which isn't as it should be. But it may be easier than you think. Isn't tomorrow the Priscilla Club day? I think so. But to get back to where we were. You don't like these family meals much, do you?"

"Not much. Not hardly at all," Matthew said. "Sometimes I think it'd be better if Sunday didn't come."

23

"But it does. And *you* can't get away."

Matthew watched as his father doubled up one fist and pounded on his knee. Then he pulled his gold watch from the pocket of his corduroy vest. "I'd better get a move on. If I was a braver man I'd stay and face the family with you."

"Could I ask you something first? Why did you say people are like leeches?"

"Not all people, Matt. Just the ones like the Spencers who didn't inherit as much money as your mother. They seem to think they have a right to feed on others — on her."

"But Mama asks *them*."

"So she does. For her own reasons. To supply her own needs I suppose," Andrew Kirk said. "I don't know as this is the kind of thing a father should say, but I'm glad you've found a hiding place."

For the rest of his life Matthew treasured the memory of that afternoon, just past three o'clock on a misty day when he was nearly nine. He saw the gold of his father's pocket watch and heard the click of the lid as it was opened with a thumbnail. He smelled the moist earth of the crib floor and felt the rough surface of the top of the wedge-shaped grains of corn. And somehow he felt less lonely — a little anyway.

3

As Matthew surveyed the first fourteen years of his life it seemed that nothing changed after he was nine except that he gradually understood more about the circumstance of his existence. This enlarged view was like the study of history which had been the leavening element in his school life from the time he entered the third grade.

He aligned himself with the discipline of lessons and regular hours and rarely complained about having to do homework. Sometimes it was a welcome excuse for going to his room. The regularity of schedule made him feel anchored in time and place and being careful to put capital letters where they were required and not to omit proper punctuation gave the blue-eyed child a sense of security.

But it was history which challenged and enlivened his mind. He wanted to know more than the books told about people like Paul Revere and Henry Clay. He was even more interested in those who were barely mentioned. He read the poem about the midnight ride of Paul Revere and wondered why no one wrote much about William Dawes. He went along on the mission of warning colonists that the British were coming overland and rode even farther than his friend. Who could be sure that one man would have made the trip? So why wasn't more said about the other rider? And how many other historical events were only partly told?

As Matthew began to dig deeper into the records of the past he also delved beneath the surface events of his own life. He'd never been told that the family could not afford to have or do anything. The amount of money at their disposal never limited him. It was his mother's will that let the family finances either trickle or flow.

Matthew couldn't pinpoint the time when he became aware that this was not the case in all families. He became aware that his father never wrote checks nor handed out money for groceries as did Garry C.'s papa.

After the talk in the corncrib Matthew saw a glimmer of reason. His father said that his mother had inherited the farms. Did this mean that Andrew Kirk didn't have any money of his own? *Does Mama give* him *money? I never saw that happen. But if she doesn't, how does he buy what he needs? Or does he?*

Most of the time Matthew replaced these puzzling questions with his own interest and activities. Because of his father's understanding he was allowed to play with Garry C. more often and even to take the neighbor boy in the house on the days when his mother attended Priscilla Club or went shopping.

The best times came when he and his father hitched Lady or Gray Dancer to the racing cart and drove either up and down the roads wherever the notion took them or directly to the oval track in the fairgrounds on the west edge of Richmond. Matthew didn't love horses. In truth he was a little afraid of them and never wanted to ride on their backs. But he loved riding in the black sulky with the canary yellow wheels. The horse's hooves clip-clopped on the gravel and sometimes sparks flew when an iron horseshoe hit the flint in large stones in the road. The rubber tired wheels whirred and the sound was not unlike the wind which swished through Matthew's light brown hair and against his face.

Part of the time he rode with his father on the trips around the dirt track. Sometimes he chose to sit or lean on the board fence and watch the other drivers who were training and pacing horses. He enjoyed the trips more when there was time for him to climb the wooden steps to the spot where a cannon was mounted on the crest of a hill. He never played war, not even when Garry C. suggested such games. Fighting wasn't fun but it was part of history. Where had this rusty weapon been used? No Civil War battles had been fought way up here in Indiana.

Matthew avoided the barns where race horses were stabled after the day he heard a couple of drivers telling a story he only partly understood and wished he hadn't heard. But there was a day when his father drove the sulky into the driveway between the rows of box stalls. A man was slouched on a bale of hay.

Andrew Kirk pulled gently on the leather lines and brought Gray Dancer to a pawing stop. "Howdy, Ray. I didn't see you out on the track. Is Chief under the weather?"

"Nope. I reckon I'm the one that's a little downsy.

27

Here. Want a swig of my medicine?"

Matthew saw the glint of glass as the man whose name was Ray pulled something out of a sagging coat pocket. *That doesn't look like any of the medicine bottles I ever saw*, he thought.

"No. No. None for me," Andrew Kirk said.

"What's a matter? On the wagon?"

"In a manner of speaking," Matthew's father said. "Well, we'd better trot back. Watch yourself."

They'd ridden about two miles before Matthew was brave enough to say, "That wasn't medicine, was it?"

"Not strictly speaking — no that's a dishonest answer. It was whiskey."

"Then why did that man call it medicine? So I wouldn't know what it really was?"

"Probably. Or to hide the fact that he was using it for what pains him — his own weakness."

Things clicked in Matthew's mind. One picture followed another like the numbered cards for the stereoptican viewer. He saw his father take the flat sided bottle from the top of a beam in the cellar. He couldn't visualize him drinking any of the amber liquid because he'd slipped upstairs without his father knowing he'd been followed.

Questions jounced around in Matthew's mind as Gray Dancer pulled the sulky up the rutted lane. What kind of pain was in his father's mind? Was it there all the time or only now and then? Did someone cause it? Or did he really hurt somewhere?

Another question erased the others as they came within sight of the house. Was his mother home? He knew it was best if they came back before she did even if he wasn't sure why. But he knew he liked it better when he wasn't asked a bunch of questions about where they'd been, who they saw, and what his father said to people they'd met.

Sometimes he wondered why his mother *didn't* ask these questions. She had to know they'd been away. But she came home lost in thoughts of where she'd been and didn't notice anyone for a while. *It's only when she has time to settle down before we get here that she seems to care what's been going on with us.*

Matthew was fourteen before he had doubts about whether or not his mother loved him. He accepted the role she played in his life as the part which a mother should fill. She was never harsh with him and it took a long time for him to wonder if this was a sign of genuine tenderness or the manner of gentility. Letitia often made audible distinctions between people who were genteel and those who were common. There were few of the former around the neighborhood. And most of the people who lived nearby were in the lower classification with the exception of all of the Spencers and two or three Kirks.

The picture Matthew had of his mother included a perfume that made it seem that lilac blossoms were always near, and of dresses or blouses with ruffly necks. She never wore plain collars and the colors of the ruffles made it seem that her face was set in flower petals, either white or pink or misty blue. He knew certain qualities of her nature and her manners even though he never spoke of what he realized. She never called herself Letitia Kirk. Spencer was always included in the identification. She never scolded him,

29

nor his father, while they were eating. Sometimes Matthew heard shrillness in her voice after he was in bed and echoes of conversation came from other parts of the house. Nor did she stay in one of her long silences during mealtime. They were recesses from her not-speaking periods. But her words at such times said little. They were part of her polite pattern. She said things like "Martha Gail seasoned the Swiss steak exactly right *this* time." Or "The mail carrier was disgustingly late — again."

Matthew always hoped that Martha Gail was listening at the swinging door when his mother said good things about the food and that she didn't hear the complaining. She'd helped with the housework since before Matthew was born. At least that's how Letitia described the duties of the solemn lady with the dark red hair which was becoming snowy with gray. Actually Martha Gail Jellison did all the housework, including the cooking and the laundry. She wasn't really friendly with Matthew, but neither was she cross. He could curl up in the high backed rocker at the end of the kitchen range and read without being made to feel he was in the way. She never shooed him out of the room when he leaned on the long worktable and watched her cut spicy dough into star-shaped ginger cookies or slice stacks of flour dusted strips into thin egg noodles.

When his mother complained that the meat was over-seasoned or the coffee strong enough to float an egg, Matthew felt a flutter of fear. He wouldn't want Martha Gail to quit or be fired. The deeper awareness about the situation in his home included the fact that his mother would have panicked if she thought she'd have to do her own work. Somehow Matt knew no one else could ever suit his mother as well. No one else had taken such constant care of Letitia Spencer from the time she was born. Martha Gail was part of his mother's inheritance.

As Matthew grew older and stronger he began to help Miss Jellison in small ways. He carried in armloads of wood that Garry C.'s father split and stacked in the shed across the brick walk from the back door of the kitchen. He picked up pans of scraps and carried them to the V-shaped trough in the chicken yard. His mother often talked about moving the flock of Buff Orphington hens to Spencer Farm, No. 2. She considered hens as necessary nuisances. She didn't like the way they looked or sounded or smelled. But the thought of using eggs that had been laid more than three days before made her shudder and she'd never buy a hen at a butcher shop. There was always the chance that it came from a diseased flock and she knew that the black tips of pinfeathers from more common varieties of chickens stained the flesh. Her mother had been the first person in the township to keep buff chickens that laid such large, pinkish-beige eggs. She often said, "Mama wouldn't have wanted me to let the strain die out."

There were few things in Matthew's home which hadn't been there when his mother's parents were alive, with the exception of the boy and his father. His mother was distressed when the lower threads began to show in the pattern of the dining room rug. She searched for one which was like the overall design of triangles and squares. She found one with the same geometric figures but had to accept a predominant color

31

of turquoise rather than burgundy.

He never forgot the time his father bought the black leather couch which curled up at one end. Matthew first saw it when he came home from school. The shiny leather glistened in the slanting rays of the late afternoon sun. The tufts were like hundreds of diamond-shaped pillows. He put his books and lunch bucket in the green wicker porch swing and sat down on the springy couch. Then he squirmed around and leaned back on the curled end. He didn't think dusty shoes would hurt this covering. Then he heard his parents. Had they been quarreling when he walked up on the porch? Or was anger making their voices louder? He couldn't hear whole sentences, only words like "rights" and "ungrateful" and "cold" and "coarse." These pieces of conversation didn't make sense but somehow they told him something. He knew the couch would never be moved into the house.

He was right. It sat on the porch for three days and when it disappeared Matthew wanted to ask if the man from the furniture store had taken it back. But before he'd decided who would want to answer he heard the hammering from the old carriage shed. This was on a Saturday morning and his mother and Aunt Lola were leaving for Indianapolis. "Don't you want to go?" Letitia asked. But Matthew could tell she wasn't saying, "I want you with me." So he said he'd rather stay at home.

"Well, I suppose it's all right," Letitia said. "At least Martha Gail will be here."

Matthew wondered what Garry C. was doing and he decided to look for his father and get permission to walk down to the tenant house. He followed the echoes of the pounding to their source. He blinked as he went into the dusky shed, and ran into the old corn sheller. When his eyes were adjusted to the dim light he saw the black leather couch ahead of him. Then he walked toward the open door which led into the harness room. His father was nailing new boards on the walls. Three were already covered. The pegs on which the harness had hung before the new horse barn was built were gone. The clean smell of new wood was in the air and golden sawdust had sifted onto the floor.

Andrew Kirk turned for another pine board. "So! I'm discovered."

"Wasn't I supposed to?"

"I didn't mean that. Wonder what I'm up to?"

"No. Not exactly," Matthew said. "You fixing up a place for the couch?"

"Right you are. It doesn't fit the Spencerian style. And maybe this is better."

"What else you going to put out here?"

"Any ideas?" Andrew asked.

"There are some chairs in the attic. I poke around up there now and then."

"I forgot all about those. They were my mother's. Have cane seats, don't they?"

"Well, they're woven of something," Matthew said. "Want me to bring them down?"

"Think you'll need any help?"

"No. They're not heavy."

By noon the walls were covered and the wide boards of the floor swept clear of debris. The couch and two chairs were all the furniture the space would allow, except for one corner.

"What could we put over there?"

"We *could* put a lot of things," his father said. "But it'll have to be a stove. The next time I win a race or a heat I'll buy a small coal burner."

Is that where he goes? Matthew wondered. *And how he earns money. At races?*

"It's a nice place," Matthew said. "Like a — "

"A hiding place?" his father said.

"Yes. I guess."

"Then feel free Matt. Come out whenever you wish — if I'm here or not."

4

For some reason he couldn't have explained at the time, Matthew didn't use the harness room as a hiding place even after what happened the week before his fourteenth birthday. This pine-walled room was his father's escape. Matthew never ran to the barn to avoid his mother's guests or sneaked through the heavy door which could be fastened both inside and out with a slide bolt of copper.

But the room with its one high window was still a place he liked to be. He spent many hours in it. After the small Florence Hot Blast stove was set up, a bucket of West Virginia coal could keep the space as warm as the giant furnace and steam radiators kept the big house.

Matthew liked to be in his father's retreat on cloudy days or dusky evenings. He curled up on the couch and watched the rosy glow of the fire through the panel of isinglass squares. As time went on he began to wonder why the fire never died out.

The room was always a little warm and if he put a couple of chunks of fuel on the fiery bed of coals he could soon take off his coat. Was his father out here more than he'd realized? He began to notice signs that showed why he hadn't heard as much conversation between his parents as usual and why his father missed so many meals. He found a folded blanket and a feather pillow on the couch and sometimes apples or crackers or cheese sat on an upturned wooden box beneath the four-paned window.

No one except his father ever found Matthew in the harness room. He wasn't sure that his mother or even Martha Gail knew that Andrew Kirk had made the space habitable. This wasn't surprising. Letitia Spencer Kirk rarely used the back door which was the only point from which she could have seen anyone enter or leave the barn. Sometimes she walked to the side yard to snip lilacs in spring or snapdragons in summer or fringed asters in autumn. Matthew looked for her before he slipped down the brick walk, through the picket gate, and up the slope to the barn.

At the time Matthew thought he'd had no warning that his life would be different after his fourteenth birthday. But looking back he could see that this was not true. The main change was that Martha Gail went out of her way to be kind to him. She asked him how school'd been when he went to the kitchen for a ginger cookie or to be with someone. And she listened while he answered her question. He didn't know how far she'd gone in school but he could tell there were some subjects which were only strange names to her. A kind of veil came over her green eyes when he mentioned algebra or geometry. But a glint of light came when he talked about poetry. "I always like it when some writer person puts feeling and sound into lines," she said. "Some verses rolls around in my mind

36

like music, makes washboard scrubbing and potato digging a little less noticeable."

After that Matthew often took his literature book, or a volume of poetry from the library, and read as Martha Gail rolled out pie dough or beat egg whites into meringue. The thumps of the rolling pin and the click of the wire whisk on the sides of the blue bowl went along with the meter of the stanzas.

"Evangeline" and "Snowbound" were Martha Gail's favorite poems. At first Matthew thought it was because Longfellow and Whittier wrote of the land and the weather and people who lived in harmony with both elements. But one snowy evening he learned why she asked to hear these works more than any other.

Letitia was gone that evening — not to be the guest of any of the people she'd entertained, but to Chicago to look for velvet the shade of the dust-worn drapes in the parlor. She would be gone for two nights and Matthew didn't expect his father to be at home either.

School was dismissed at two that afternoon because an east wind was swirling snow into drifts and the horses might have a hard time pulling hacks through some places. The hedge fences on Shockley's road made a tunnel into which wind-whipped snow was driven.

Matthew was shivering when he opened the front door. The front part of the house was chilly. The hissing, clanking radiators could not neutralize the cold that seeped around the east and north windows. Matthew hurried upstairs and changed his clothes before clattering downstairs and through the hall to the kitchen. He walked softly when his mother was at home.

Martha Gail was standing at the side door. Matthew was surprised. She was usually busy. Did his mother's absence change things for everyone?

"Grandpa's sure letting the feathers fly today," she said.

Matthew knew what she meant. Even though she wasn't talkative, snow always brought an echo of her childhood to her mind. She never failed to say, "I see Grandma's picking her geese and Grandpa's throwing the feathers away," when she spied a snowflake sifting through the air.

"I know," Matthew said. "I've been out in it. The drift at the curve of the lane came all the way to my knees."

"Did you get in over your boots?"

"Yes. But I emptied them before much melted."

"We're liable to be snowed in by ourselves," Martha Gail said. "I don't see any signs of a letup. 'Less your Papa makes it back."

"Does that scare you?"

"No. No reason to be afraid. We got plenty of provisions, and there's wood in the shed and coal in the cellar. What sounds tasty for supper?"

"I don't remember that you ever asked me that before," Matthew said.

"Good reason. There's always been someone to tell me."

Matthew sat down in the high backed rocker and put his feet on the open oven door. The heat generated by burning wood mixed with chunks of coal covered him like a blanket.

"You didn't say what you wanted to eat."

"How about fried potatoes — crusty. Like when Mama calls them burned."

"Easy enough," Martha Gail said. "And I went ahead and made some float. It's cooling in the snow."

"What's float?"

"Custard — thin egg custard. My ma made it. In warm weather it was custard. Cooled in snow it was float."

"I don't see much sense in that," Matthew said.

"Me neither. I just keep on saying it anyhow." As she took potatoes from a basket in the cellarway she asked, "You got lessons to do?"

"No."

"I was thinking. This would be a fitting time to hear the snow poem. If you don't mind taxing your throat for my pleasure."

"I don't mind." He'd found a book of American poetry in the attic and slipped it behind the mantel clock.

Martha Gail moved and worked without making much noise. She pulled the cast-iron skillet to the lids behind the firebox when the grease began to hiss and sputter. And she slipped a blue granite cover over the potatoes to muffle the splattering.

Matthew read slowly when he came to phrases like: "Shut in from the world without, we sat the clean winged hearth about." The words gave him a feeling of safety.

Martha Gail interrupted him when he came to the stanzas which dealt with the stories told around the red logs. "These taters are just right. I reckon we'd better finish the reading later." She didn't ask if

Matthew wanted to eat in the kitchen. She seemed to know he wouldn't want to sit alone in the high-ceilinged dining room. She spread a red-and-white checked cloth over the end of the long worktable and used the ironstone plates which were imprinted with a single gold leaf.

She was pouring foamy hot chocolate into thick cups when they heard the stomping of feet at the side door. As they turned to see who'd made it through the drifts, Andrew Kirk called, "Don't be alarmed, Mrs. Jellison."

"My sakes alive!" Martha Gail said. "I wasn't looking for you. Not so soon anyhow."

"Well. I kept wondering how you two were getting along. I tried to call. Or didn't you know the telephone's out of order?"

"No. I don't pay much attention to it. Most of the time I don't even hear the fool thing ring. It being in the front rooms."

"You have any trouble getting up the lane, Matt?"

"No. But I might have — if my legs had been shorter or the drifts higher. How'd you get through?"

"I went around, followed the valley along the creek."

"That's a long ways," Martha Gail said. "No wonder you're plastered with snow. You get into dry duds while I rustle up some supper."

"No fuss. I'll have what you're having," Matthew's father said as he started toward the stairs.

"Maybe he will and maybe he won't," Martha Gail said. "I'll have to slice a couple of more potatoes into the skillet, and maybe scramble a few hen-berries. Being out in all that cold builds up an appetite."

The three, who'd never eaten together in the kitchen or any other place, lingered for over an hour. Martha Gail made the second pan of hot chocolate and the bowl of float was all gone by the time they'd had second helpings. The wind seemed to grow stronger. It swished snow against the windowpanes and whistled around the corner of the house. Andrew and Matthew made two trips across the brick walk to the woodshed and piled split sticks of hickory and elm in the box at the end of the kitchen range.

Prince, the border collie, followed them into the kitchen. He was shivering and his black and white coat was frosted with ice and snow. "What's wrong?" Andrew Kirk asked as he stooped to scratch the dog's head. "The wind drive the snow through your doghouse? Would it upset you if we let him sleep here tonight, Mrs. Jellison?"

"Not me," Martha Gail said. "I'm not the one that made the rule about him being shut outdoors."

Matthew curled up on the braided rug and rubbed the dog's coat with a worn towel. Before long Prince stopped shaking and stretched out into sleep. Matthew was having trouble keeping his eyes open when his father spoke. "Your room will be warm Mrs. J., but Matt's will be like an icebox being on the east. How would you like it if we pulled a mattress downstairs and slept here in the kitchen? That way I can keep this fire going."

"I'd like it," Matthew said.

Tugging on the unwieldy roll of bedding erased the drowsiness for a while. But after the lights were out he was sleepy again. He could hear the crackling of the sparking fire and the even breathing of Prince. The wind still whistled and puffed but none of these sounds made him uneasy.

He was drifting into unconsciousness when a thought jerked him awake. "Papa. Why do you call Martha Gail Mrs. Jellison?"

"That's her name."

"But no one else calls her that. And I never even heard she was married."

"She was. But not for long. Her husband was your grandfather's hired man — a term I hate. But no matter about that now. He was sent up a ladder on Farm No. 2, in spite of the fact that heights terrified him. He fell from the top of the silo. That was just before your mother and I were married. I've always felt Mrs. J. came here because she couldn't bear to stay in the little tenant house. And that she'd not have come here if Aaron Spencer hadn't moved to the city. But — maybe I shouldn't tell you this, she never spoke to your grandfather from that time until his death."

"She doesn't talk much to anyone," Matthew said. "But lately she says more to me. A lot more."

"That's good. That's good."

"Maybe that's why Martha Gail likes to hear me read about 'Evangeline' and from 'Snowbound.' "

"What's why?"

"Maybe it reminds her of someone or maybe of better times."

"Probably," his father said. "I didn't know you read to her. Do you often?"

"Sometimes. When she's in the mood."

The sticks of wood shifted and pinpoint sparks shot

through the slots in the door and winked out in the shadowed light.

"I like being snowbound," Matthew said.

"You do?"

"Yes. I guess the storm outside makes being warm seem better."

5

The wind blew until sunrise the next morning but the roads were not open to traffic until thirty hours after the snow had been swirled into sculptured drifts. Matthew felt as if the farmhouse and barns were on an island of white. He and his father and Martha Gail were cut off from the world as it had been. Neither the telephone repairman nor the mail carrier could set up communication.

This time of isolation was a brief period of unusual freedom for Matthew. There were no guests, for a change. Martha Gail didn't object when he kept his boots near the kitchen stove so they'd always be warm. And she never complained because the smell of drying wool gloves was always in the air. They didn't eat a single meal in the dining room, even after the wind died down and the clanking radiators could warm the whole house.

The sun came out shortly after noon and the wintry air was like pale and misty silver. As Andrew Kirk finished eating a stack of cornmeal pancakes he said, "I think I'll hitch Gray Dancer to the stone boat. Want to go along to see Garry C.?"

"Sure," Matthew said. "But will the horse be able

to get through the drifts?"

"Not on the road. We'll cross the pasture and cut back to the road beyond the bend."

Purplish shadows were creeping across the snow by the time they headed home. Matthew's father had helped the tenant haul hay to feeder cattle in the tramp shed on the ridge. And the men had worked for over an hour thawing a waterline which ran from the pump under the windmill tower to the round tank of wooden staves.

The two boys climbed up and down the rounded ridge taking turns at pulling one another on the long sled. Their weight finally packed the snow into an icy path. And the downward swoops made each uphill climb worth the energy and breath they took.

When they came to the snow-filled section of the road on the way home they could see that no wheel tracks were traced on the surface. "The snowplow's not been through here," Andrew said.

Matthew took a deep breath of relief. He liked the feeling of his home. He didn't dislike his mother. *But when she's here none of us are the same. Papa's not around as much. And Martha Gail doesn't smile. I don't know for sure how I'm different. Except I keep wondering what my parents are thinking — about each other.*

They did the chores by lantern that night. The fan-shaped flame of gold wavered and flickered as they moved. Shadows danced and bobbed. The barn was warm in comparison to the outdoor temperature which dropped to three below zero by sundown. The cows in the stalls and the sheep in their pens nibbled and munched in comfort. Matthew chopped eight ears of corn into three-inch chunks for the horses.

"I'm almost hungry enough to eat some of this corn," Matthew said as he held the lantern high so his father could see to bolt the barn door.

"I imagine Martha Gail's taken that possibility under advisement," Andrew said as they followed the gleam of light from the kitchen window.

"Sometimes you sound like my history teacher," Matthew said.

"I do?"

"Yes. Once in a while." He didn't go ahead and say, "When Mama's not around," but that's what he thought.

Andrew spoke as they leaned against the house to take off their snow-encrusted boots. "That's not too surprising. That's the path I followed. For a while."

"I didn't know that. You mean you wanted to teach school?"

"I did. Even went part of a year to the normal school. That was the year before I came here."

Martha Gail was ladling thick vegetable soup into bowls. Steam curled upward in the lamplit room.

"Is my nose telling the truth?" Andrew asked. "Have you baked bread?"

"Yes. I did," Martha Gail said. "Somehow this weather seems right for home baking."

"Now Mrs. Jellison. I know you. To you any time's right for baking. I see the look on your face when you serve what's bought at the store."

"I serve what I'm told," Martha Gail said. "'Cepting times like this."

46

After the table was cleared and while the dishes were being washed Matthew and his father filled the woodbox and then went to the basement to stoke the furnace with coal. Before they started upstairs Andrew said, "I'd like to talk to you Matt. Want to listen?"

Matthew didn't know what to say. He could listen, but would he like what he was about to hear? Something told him he might not. *Maybe it's the way Papa's forehead is wrinkled into an arch or how he keeps crooking his little finger.* He sat down on the wooden step, the third one from the cellar floor.

His father hesitated and then he perched on a round chunk of thornwood. "This is not easy for me, Matt," he said. "And there's no way that I can see of making it understandable to you. But being snowbound has given me time to think. At first — actually for a long time — I considered not telling you — of just going."

"Going?"

"Yes. Of not living here any more."

Matthew was aware of a little jerking feeling in his chest. It only lasted for a second or two.

"Do you want to know why?"

"You sound like you don't want to tell me."

"It's not that — no, that's not honest. I can't tell you without talking against your mother. *That's* what I'd rather not do."

"It's all right," Matthew said. "I mean about not telling me. I already understand a little."

"Like what?"

"Like her having the money and you liking horses and — well you're — so different."

"True," his father said. "It's a shame we didn't take

47

time to make that discovery before we married. But —
if we had, you wouldn't be."

Matthew had to say, "Would that have been so bad
— for you two I mean?"

His father doubled one fist and thudded into the palm
of the other hand. The thumping was not unlike a
pounding heartbeat. Finally he said in a voice
choked with pain, "Is that how we've made you feel?
As if you are not important?"

"Sometimes, yes," Matthew said. "Especially Mama.
Always having company and wanting the house to
be so fine — and neat."

"And me? How do you feel about me? About my
part in your life?"

"It's not the same — as with Mama. It's just that
you're gone a lot."

"But not because of you. And that's partly why I
made up my mind."

"I don't understand."

"It's like this. As long as I'm here I'll be living in
Letitia's house, on Spencer money, and my relation-
ship with you will be determined by her decisions.
Do you see that?"

Matthew nodded. He and his father never talked
freely if his mother was within hearing distance. They
went no place together unless she was away. He didn't
know why this was true. But it was.

"If I leave and your mother asks for a divorce,
which I figure she will, then we may be able to be
together — perhaps not more than now but with more
freedom. I am your father, Matt. And that's the only
claim I'll ever make. Not for Letitia's money — which

she thinks I want, or not even for the few head of livestock I've bought or the improvements I've made. But the right to be with you or have you come to visit me — I'll do anything for that. Even come back here if that's all I can hope for."

"Come back from where?"

"From Richmond," his father said. "I have a job working for Mr. Clark — you know, he raises and races horses."

"You'll live there?"

"Yes. I can. In two rooms. Above a harness room this time, not in it."

"You going to take the couch?"

"Not if you want it."

"No," Matthew said. "I wouldn't go out there much if you weren't around."

"There'll be room for you where I am," Andrew said. "Always. In the summer maybe you can come on long visits. Go to county fairs when it's racing season. Would you like that?"

"I think so. Anyhow I'd like being on Clark's horse farm if that's where you're working."

Andrew pulled his watch out of his vest pocket. "Martha Gail's probably wondering what we're doing down here."

"I don't hear her walking around. Maybe she's gone to bed."

"Let's go upstairs and see."

The kitchen was warm but Martha Gail was not in sight. She'd left two pieces of apple pie on the table. Matthew took his and curled up on the braided rug in front of the stove and his father sat down in the rocker.

After a few minutes Andrew said, "I'm a little surprised, Matt. You don't seem upset about what I've been saying."

"I'm not. At first I felt a little funny. Sometimes changes scare me."

"They frighten all of us. But go on."

"There's not much to say. The only difference I can see is that things might be a lot better for you and more fun for me — part of the time."

The ringing of the telephone startled them. Had it always been so jangly? "Should I answer?" Matthew asked. "It must be Mama."

"I'll answer it," his father said. "I've not turned tail and run yet." He came back to the kitchen and said, "It was the operator checking to see if we heard the ring. The line was down way up on the pike. The lineman found the break late today."

Matthew wondered if his mother would call. She might not. She'd think repairs couldn't be made after dark.

"I think I'll go in and listen to the phonograph awhile," Andrew Kirk said.

"I'll come too, but I'm getting sleepy."

He propped his head up with two green velvet pillows. He couldn't remember ever going to sleep on this couch before. It was scratchier than the daybed in the dining room where he slept when he had a cold or the time he had old-fashioned measles.

The phonograph record whirled until the needle moved into the groove where music had been imprinted.

Before Matthew drifted into sleep he said, "Papa. I

don't know anyone who's been divorced. Do you?"

"Not out here," Andrew said. "Will that worry you? What people will say?"

"No," Matthew said. "I don't pay much attention."

"Good policy. But it may be that I've misjudged your mother. She may care more about what people say than about being sure she's free of any claims I might make."

Matthew didn't open his eyes until snow-brightened sunshine came in the long east window. He'd slept on the couch all night in his clothes. Someone, probably his father, had covered him with a puffy comforter. Martha Gail would have sent him up to bed.

He locked his hands behind his head and yawned. Waking up in this room was like being in a strange place. He wrinkled his nose trying to decide what Martha Gail was cooking. It wouldn't be pancakes. They'd had them the day before. Then Mrs. Jellison called from the hall, "Omelets baking. And they don't wait on sleepyheads."

Matthew took three stairs at a time on his way up for a pair of clean socks. He was halfway down when the telephone rang. He knew who he'd hear before he took the black receiver from the hook.

6

Andrew Kirk left the farm a week later but he and Letitia were never divorced. Another kind of separation loosened her grip on life and she died seventeen months after the bank foreclosed on the two mortgages.

Matthew was aware that they'd moved to the city because the flag of his mother's pride was lowered. She couldn't bear living near people who'd always known her. And he realized that she'd salvaged very little of what she'd inherited from her father. That's why they moved into half of a double house on the edge of town. But he didn't understand what had happened to the money until Aunt Lola told him what she called the blunt truth.

His mother's cousin moved to the city with them, while Martha Gail stayed on to work for the new owners. Matthew missed her but somehow he knew she'd be happier if she stayed, perhaps more so than she'd been for years. He also could see why Aunt Lola chose to live with them. She'd been at the farm a lot of the time anyway and she was the only person in the world who could tell Letitia anything. She was a source of strength now.

Matthew wasn't upset by any of the upheaval except

for the fact that he wouldn't see Garry C. very often, if ever. He liked the new neighborhood. The streets were narrow but shady and they were only two blocks from the park. The streetcars stopped at the corner half a square away, and he went to the library two or three times a week, even during the months when school was in session.

From the beginning it was Aunt Lola he asked if it was all right if he explored in the park or went uptown. His mother was in the darkened upstairs bedroom a lot. Her sick headaches lasted longer now. One afternoon, seven weeks after they left the farm, Matthew went to the latticed back porch where Lola Allen was sewing patches on the elbows of one of his shirts.

"Isn't Mama any better?" he asked. "She hasn't been down for two days. Looks like she'd be hungry by now."

"Don't fret. She's not starving," Lola said. "She says she can't stand the sight of food. But she eats all I tote up the stairs. Of course I take what she orders."

Then Lola Allen said, "Matthew, why do you keep on calling me aunt? You know I'm not, don't you?"

"Sure. But Mama always told me to call any of her folks aunt or uncle."

"Well. It's all right I guess. But I'd just as soon you called me by my name. It's more friendly. And I figure you and I could use some friendliness about now."

Neither spoke for a while. A horse's hooves clip-clopped, and wheels gritted on the cinder alley. A soft breeze moved the clematis vine and it whispered on the crisscrossed lath.

"Got lots of questions in your mind, Matt? About all that's happened?"

"About some. Not about Papa though. He talked to me."

"That's good," Lola Allen said. "You'll be seeing him."

"When?"

"Next Friday. But go on. I didn't give you a chance to say what you don't understand."

"What happened to the money? Why did the bank take over the farm?"

"I reckon that's mystified a lot of people — but not me nor your father. The blunt truth is there never was as much as people thought. Not by a long ways."

She told Matthew that his grandfather had made many bad investments. He had bought stock in companies which either failed or didn't exist. Then he borrowed more money, took out second mortgages, and left things pretty shaky.

"Your mother wouldn't face facts. She'd not been brought up to do that. My ma said she was raised like a jewel in a cottonlined case. She wouldn't let your father make any decisions and the ones she made got her farther and farther in debt."

"Are we poor?" Matthew asked.

"Not to my way of thinking," Lola said. "There was enough left to keep this double house your granddad owned. Rent from the other half will provide you with food and the other necessities. And there were some bonds. They'll bring in a little interest. If your mother doesn't decide to sell them and live high again."

Letitia Spencer Kirk never made such a decision. She couldn't adjust to living within an income. Her will to live flickered and failed and she became a victim of an epidemic of grippe and pneumonia.

By this time Lola Allen had assumed an important role in Matthew's life. Sometimes he felt he'd never really known her before. Or was she different when her cousin was around? Was his father right when he said Lola had lived in Letitia's shadow?

Andrew Kirk and Lola talked for nearly a whole day the Sunday after the funeral. They insisted that Matthew take a part in the discussion. "It concerns you, son," Andrew said. "And we want you to have your say."

They told him that the property was his and that he either could live in it with his cousin or go with his father. "Do I have to decide right now?" he asked.

"What do you mean?" Lola Allen asked.

"Well, if you are going to live here and Papa where he is, couldn't we sort of let it work out?"

"Certainly," his father said. "But what do you want to do?"

"Both," Matthew said. "I like this place and the school. But I like going with you too."

"Then that's how it will be," Andrew said. "Lola says she's willing to make a home for you."

Matthew didn't like the word willing. He was wishing for more when Lola said, "It's stronger than that, Andrew. This boy is as close to being my own child as I've ever had or ever will. I'd hate to live here or anywhere else without having him around — at least part of the time."

Tears welled up in Matthew's eyes and he let them

roll down on his cheeks. For the first time in years he didn't try to hide them. Even during the funeral his eyes had been dry when others were around. And he'd held back sobs until he was alone on the daybed in the dining room. Now he felt a new freedom, or was this being natural?

Lola moved into Letitia's room after she papered the walls in sprigs of daffodils. "It's a shame to cover up wallpaper that's only been on a year," she said, "but blue makes me moody."

There were almost no melancholy times in Matthew's life for the next few years. He soon made friends and never hesitated about them to come to the house. But he didn't crave company and many Sundays he and Lola ate alone, except for the days his father came.

Before he was a senior in high school he knew he wanted to be a teacher and that history was the subject he liked to talk about most when he thought anyone wanted to listen. He didn't know if there was enough money for him to take some training, but was almost sure he'd find some way to go to college.

The way and the place seemed to unfold as graduation time came closer. When Matthew's father heard what his son wanted to do a new light seemed to shine in his eyes. The two of them were sitting on top of the board fence around an oval racetrack in Greenville, Ohio, when Matthew said he'd like to go to college when fall came.

"Why didn't you tell me this before?" Andrew asked. "So we could make plans."

"I guess I figured it was up to me mainly."

"That's true. About where to go. Or if. But I've

saved up some money. And I'd like to have a stake in this."

Matthew remembered that his father had meant to teach history. Was this the reason he was willing to help? *What if I wanted to do something else. Like being a lawyer? Or a doctor, as Mama wanted?*

His father answered the unspoken questions. He did this more often as they spent more time together. "Whatever you decide to do it's the same. I can give you a boost. You aiming to go to school here? To Earlham?"

"Yes, sir. It's a good place. And it'd cost less. Besides, Lola will like the idea of me staying around."

"That's true," Andrew said. "She's made a good home for you. I appreciate that. I reckon you know you could get a certificate by passing an examination?"

"I know. But I'd feel better if I learned more before trying to teach others."

Neither spoke for a while. Then Matthew said, "Sometimes I wonder something about Lola. She's a lot older than Mama. But she seems young — in her thinking."

"For example?"

"In lots of ways," Matthew said. "She's probably seen millions of spider webs. But lots of mornings she calls me to the backyard to see how the dew's like pearls on all the strands."

"She sees the wonder of the world in which she lives."

"She sure does. And she helps me see things I never noticed before. She's always comparing things like the moon."

"The *moon*?"

"Yes. Sometimes it looks like an up-tipped canoe to her. Or a silver toenail in the sky. Last week she could see it faintly in the daytime sky. She called it a dandelion that had gone to seed and said a puff of wind might blow it into the air."

As they'd talked, pacers and trotters pulled two-wheeled sulkys around and around the dirt track. "Any out there fast enough to beat Mr. Clark's horses?" Matthew asked.

"Some can and some can't," Andrew said. "But I don't see many with enough speed to outspace Single J."

"Single J.?"

"Got a little surprise for you. Come back to the stable and I'll introduce you to our horse."

On the way he explained that he'd bought a colt that Mr. Clark had considered a cull. "He didn't look like much for a while. Kind of knob-kneed. But I liked the way he moved. And I could afford what Mr. Clark said he was worth."

"Why didn't you tell me?" Matthew asked.

"Self-protection I guess," his father said. "I could have been wrong. And if it turned out I'd made a bad deal I wouldn't have had to admit it to anyone — except myself."

"You think you've got a good thing?"

"I think so. This Tuesday we'll know. He's entered in the second race. That's why I sort of insisted you stay two or three nights. To help me and to see Single J.'s first race."

Matthew still didn't share his father's love for horses

58

but he enjoyed the excitement and even the work of grooming the silver-gray animal. He held the halter as his father trimmed the forelock and mane. "I see where his name comes from. That mark on his face does look like a J."

The horse didn't win his first race but he came in second. "Are you disappointed?" Matthew asked as he helped rub the horse's silvery coat.

"No," Andrew said. "I didn't expect to do this well. Not on the first time out. Barring trouble this gray will help us build up a nest egg. Maybe I'll have my own stable sooner'n I figured. But first we're going to get your feet on the path."

"You don't seem upset about waiting," Matthew said.

"Nope! Some things are worth the waiting. And there's another thing. I've learned a lot working here. And what this experience has taught me will keep me from wasting what it's taking years to earn. I'd probably have made all kinds of mistakes if I'd had the free use of money to have bought my own place outright."

7

Within three months Matthew became a part of another family on a now-and-then basis. His father came over on a cold and rainy evening to tell Lola and Matt that he was going to get married the next Sunday. Rushes of wind drove the late October rain against the windowpanes and sometimes a downdraft sent puffs of woodsmoke through the cracks around the door of the heating stove.

"East winds always do that," Lola said. "That's why I don't burn coal when the gusts come from that direction."

"That might cause a little problem in below zero weather," Andrew said. "Wood fires don't throw out as much heat."

"We got that situation in hand," Lola said. "We sit around the kitchen range. The roof's flat out there and the wind doesn't play any such tricks."

Matthew was polishing his oxblood shoes. He'd been attending the small frame church over on South B Street and intended to go the next morning if his father didn't stay all night. Andrew, as far as his son knew, never went to church. He never said anything against the institution and he knew a lot about the Bi-

60

ble. Evidence of this knowledge often appeared in his conversation. Sometimes he'd glance up at the hills of southern Indiana which rose beyond some of the county fair racetracks. He'd draw a deep breath and say, "I will lift my eyes unto the hills from which cometh my strength." He often compared the beauty of nature to apples of gold in pictures of silver. A redwing blackbird could be the apple and a flowering honeysuckle vine its silver frame.

No one had spoken for two or three minutes. The fire sizzled dampness out of the hickory chunks and Matthew's brush whisked against his high-topped shoes.

"Anyone hungry?" Lola asked. "There's a raspberry pie left over, and I made a batch of hermits this morning. Used black walnuts this time. They're more flavorful than hickory nuts."

"We've not had time to get hungry," Andrew said. "At least I haven't. And I have to head back shortly."

Matthew asked, "You aren't spending the night?"

"Nope. Not this time. And probably not often again, if ever."

Matthew glanced at Lola Allen. She looked as surprised as he felt. Before either found words to form a question Andrew said. "I'll be putting my feet under my own table in a manner of speaking. I'm getting married in another week."

He told them that his wife-to-be was a widow, whose name was Inez Newton. Her husband had been killed seven years before and she'd been left to finish bringing up three children. "She does sewing for folks and has all the work she can manage. But it's not a high-paying occupation."

"Where will you live?" Lola asked.

"Over by New Castle," Andrew said. "Mr. Clark has a farm there. He decided to build it up — make another horse farm instead of adding buildings here. I'll be on the shares."

"How old are her children?" Matt asked.

"Well, the oldest, Ellen, is about your age. She was around ten when her papa was killed. The other girl and a boy stairstep down from her."

Neither Matthew nor Lola Allen asked how long Andrew had known Mrs. Newton. Somehow Matthew sensed that if his father had wanted them to know he would have told them. But he couldn't help wondering, *Is this the reason Papa was away from the farm so often — one of them anyway?*

"Well, Andrew," Lola said. "I hope this is a good move. I'd say you're due."

Andrew's mouth quirked at one corner in the start of a smile. "Thank you, Lola." Then he turned to Matthew. "Now, you're welcome to join up with this new household either regular or part time."

"I'd better stay here," Matthew said, "on account of school and to look after Lola or to keep on letting her take care of me."

"I figured you'd say that," Andrew said. "But the offer's open. Now I reckon I'd better head back. The horse I'm driving doesn't exactly have cat's eyes."

"When do we get to meet this special lady?" Lola asked.

Andrew rubbed a knuckle across an eyebrow and grinned. "I guess I was more fidgety about breaking the news than I realized. She — Inez — wants you to

62

eat dinner at her place tomorrow. I can come get you and bring you back."

"I reckon we could ride the streetcar," Lola said. "Or does it go anyways near?"

"Yes. Take the Congerville car and get off at 13th Street. Inez lives in the yellow story-and-a-half house three doors south. There's a side porch and a brick walk. I'll be there ahead of you."

Matthew pulled back the door curtain and watched until his father drove down the rain blackened street and went out of sight. He turned to see that his cousin had left the room. Then he heard the clatter of pans. "What are you dong?" he asked as he walked into the kitchen.

"I'm going to stir up a Lord Baltimore cake," she said. "You don't think I'm going to go over there empty-handed? But — you *don't* know, do you? That I always took something when I went to visit your mother when you lived out on the farm."

Matthew was bewildered. Somehow he had the idea that Lola sponged off his mother. He didn't hold it against her. He knew she'd made herself useful, had done patching, and made lace doilies for her cousin.

"No," Lola said. "I was bound and determined not to be a leech. But your mother needed someone to stand up to her and no one else did. It never had much effect, but I kept trying and aimed to pay my way with jars of strawberry preserves and comb honey and Lord Baltimore cakes. They're your papa's favorite."

Matthew went back to the sitting room and picked up a book. But his thoughts and the author's sentences were jumbled. *I've thought for a long time that Lola liked Papa — more than Mama. She always stood up for him. Lately I've had the idea he and Lola might get married. Did she think the same? Is she upset?*

He'd begun to dread the next day. Now his feelings became less self-centered. If Lola was disappointed she was going right on with the plan to meet his father's new family. Seeing how she might be feeling lessened his own uneasiness.

The skies cleared during the night and Sunday was a perfect example of October's bright blue weather. The air was cool but still. None of the fallen leaves stirred except when they were moved by footsteps. Matthew went to Sunday school but didn't stay for worship service. The rain of the day before had washed the dust of summer from the world he saw. The white weatherboarding of the church glistened in the sunshine and the arched windows on the east side caught the glinting rays.

Matthew always felt restored by attending church but not always for the same reason. Sometimes the words of a part of the responsive reading illumined his mind. Often the music lifted his spirits. But usually it was the time of quiet meditation which brought a comforting hush to his thoughts. In such stillness he felt God's presence.

Lola was ready to leave when he returned from church. The cake with sugary fruit and nut filling between its three layers was in the two-handled basket. Matthew started to pick it up. "Go easy," Lola said. "That icing's still a little sticky. Don't tip the basket either way."

They walked to the car stop and waited nearly ten

minutes before the lumbering trolley came from the direction of uptown. Lola operated by the theory that it was better to be early than left behind.

"You nervous?" Lola asked before the car jounced to a stop.

Matthew nodded. "A little. Can't help wondering how this will change things, I guess."

"I know," Lola said. "It all depends on whether we hit it off with this Mrs. Newton. If we don't we won't see much of your papa. He'll have to go her way. More or less. Or he should."

Andrew Kirk had the door open before they stepped onto the narrow porch. "You made it," he said. "Good for you."

"No great accomplishment," Lola said. "Since we got on the right car and got off at the right place."

A tall woman with high-piled hair stepped to the open door. "Come in," she said. "I'm Inez."

"I figured so," Lola said. "We're Matthew and Lola. I reckon you can tell one from the other."

Matthew noticed that Mrs. Newton's copper hair was dusted with white. It showed in the waves above her ears and streaked the braids that circled the crown of her head.

"These are my children," Inez said. Matthew blinked. The room seemed shadowed coming in from the silver-glinted sunlight. "This is Ellen," Inez went on, "and her sister Ann and her brother John."

The two younger children were nearly the same size, near enough alike to be twins. Either one was small for his age, and the other large, or a little of both. Their sister was almost as tall as her mother and the coppery shade of her hair was the same or maybe a little brighter — more burnished.

Before the day was over Matthew felt at ease, especially around Ellen Newton. He'd never had a sister and had not thought much about how it would feel to play the role of a brother. Yet he sensed that this hazel-eyed girl would always be direct and honest, at least with him. She wasn't flirty or didn't seem to be trying to impress him.

The younger Newton children seemed to live in a world of their own. They asked to be excused from the table while the others were eating second pieces of the fluffy cake. "They found a kite in the attic and want to see if it will fly," Mrs. Newton said.

"I doubt if there's enough wind," Andrew said.

"I think they know that," Inez answered. "But when one gets an idea the other chimes in. Supporting each other is more important to them than succeeding."

"That's unusual," Lola said. "For a brother and sister to be so close."

"John was a twin," Inez said. "James died when he was five. Of scarlet fever. It was almost more than Johnny could bear. Until he made his little sister a substitute playmate." Tears welled in her eyes.

Matthew glanced at his father. He saw a new tenderness in his eyes. Was this what he'd missed? The gentle influence? A loving relationship? At that moment all Matthew's misgivings about his father's marriage melted, like mist before sunshine.

The marriage and the move to New Castle made little change in Matthew's daily life. He and Lola went on about the same except for the fact that they had five guests instead of one on Sunday and they sometimes went to the farm east of New Castle for visits.

Another new emphasis became apparent to Matthew. Ellen Newton began to seem like his sister. They talked about their earlier lives and made comparisons. One of these conversations came on a day in May when spring had resurrected Indiana from winter. Andrew had coaxed them to go to the horse barn and he and John were leading horses around the small dirt track. Lola and Inez sat on two upended chunks of wood while Ellen and Matt leaned on the whitewashed board fence.

"You're getting white on your sweater, Ellie," Matt said.

"I know," the tall girl said. "But I like leaning. That's partly what fences are for."

The soft breeze swept puffs of dust from the track and let them fall in other places. The new leaves of an old pear tree were tufts of pale green on its lacy black branches. "You know something," Ellie said, "I've always hated to be called Ellie. Before now."

"How's now different?"

"I don't know. And I'd probably feel like slapping my other brother or sister if they nicknamed me."

"Your *other* brother?"

"That's what I mean. So rest easy. I'm not going to make eyes at you or anything — even though you are handsome enough to be conceited, which you're not, and in spite of being so tall and having such dreamy blue eyes."

Matthew grinned but didn't blush. He believed Ellie and *was* at ease around her from then on.

8

Matthew's original plan was to go to the Quaker college at Earlham just long enough to get a teaching certificate. He changed his mind for two reasons. A way of paying for tuition and books unfolded, and he felt more comfortable in the academic atmosphere than he had anywhere else in all of his nearly eighteen years. He concentrated hard on getting the most from his college experience.

He literally stumbled onto the opportunity to earn money to pay part of his expenses. He walked over to the park one Saturday afternoon in early August. The summer rainfall had been unusually heavy and the grass was still springy and green, not dry and matted. The elephant-ear leaves of the cannas were glossy, as if they'd been waxed, not limp and coated with the dust of summer.

Matthew heard the call of a bird from somewhere in a white birch tree. He circled the silver-splotched trunk, looking upward, and stumbled over a fallen limb.

"Hurt yourself?" someone asked.

"No. Just jarred me up a little," Matthew said. He brushed encrusted mud off his moleskin trousers before he looked up to see a tall man a few yards away.

"I was just comin' to clear away the storm's leavings," the man said.

"You work here?"

"I do. But I never get done. Specially when the wind sashays through the trees like last night."

Matthew watched as the man put a sharp-toothed saw on a stump and began swinging the ax at the thick branch. The leaves trembled and the limb bounced with every thud, and pale yellow wood chips danced in the air before they fell to the ground. As the man hacked sections from the limb, Matthew pulled them out of the way and stacked them on a rise in the ground.

"Know a little about cording wood, I see," the man said as he stopped to mop his forehead with a blue bandanna handkerchief.

"Yes. I lived on a farm." A flood of memories came to Matthew. He recalled going to the woods with Garry C. and his father and hauling firewood to the house on a stoneboat and stacking it by the back door to be used for cooking. A wave of homesickness surged through his thoughts and he resolved to go out and see Martha Gail the next day. She might know where Garry C. was now and what he was doing.

"Want a job?" the man said as he cut off the last portion.

"Well yes. I do. Part of the time. I'm going to Earlham this fall. But I need to work when I can."

"Come over to the office Monday. If I'm not there ask someone where I am."

"Thanks," Matthew said. "But who will I ask for?"

"Didn't say, did I? Most folks don't care. I'm just the park handyman. But my name's Dunn. Art Dunn. But it don't fit."

"What do you mean?"

"The name — I'm never done."

Matthew worked in the park until he graduated from college and for the summer following that. He didn't enjoy all the tasks but he liked working outside. And he found that he'd learned much by watching Garry C.'s father and the other farmhands. *Some people might have thought I had my nose in a book or was hiding from company most of the time, but I seem to have picked up some knowledge as I went along, perhaps by osmosis.*

During his college years Matthew became aware that in some ways he'd never change. He began to realize the quality of his own nature, to recognize his individuality. And he was comfortable about this inner view as well as with the attitude he had about others. Sometimes he felt as if he was looking at every situation as if he were either on the outside, or sitting in a place where he could see the whole scene spread out below his perch.

He first became aware of this fact of his nature in a classroom. He had one history professor who liked to shock students into thinking by making statements aimed at arousing controversy. Matthew neither reacted nor responded at first. He listened to those who did both, picked what seemed true for him, and usually made a kind of summing-up statement before the bell rang. He learned from the process of observing.

This same professor wanted Matthew to teach in the

college and he seriously considered this idea. But he realized that the reason for staying would not be healthy for him. He'd seen others who felt so safe in the cloister of college that they never assumed responsibility. Those who could afford to do so became perpetual students.

"But you'd be teaching — getting paid," Lola said when they discussed his future.

"I know. But I'd be staying for another reason. And I know it. I have to get out and see if I can use what I've been learning. And I think I'd be better with high school age pupils. Maybe I'll go back to Earlham after I prove something to myself."

"The question is," Lola said, "back from where? And will you? Folks begin to branch off and they don't seem to be able to find their way back — or don't want to retrace their steps." She was relieved when Matthew was hired to teach in the local high school. "That means you'll be around until some girl catches your eyes — and you."

"I've not met one yet that could make me as good a home as you do," Matthew said. "I'm comfortable."

"I never knew of anyone who came out and said they got married for *comfort*. And if they did they often got a good fooling."

Matthew had made some observations about marriage but he never voiced an opinion on the subject. He realized that he'd not only had a one-sided view but also a limited opportunity to assess the advantages and disadvantages. He asked a few girls to go out with him and he saw two of them more than a dozen times. But he never felt quite at ease. Some talked too much. That wouldn't have bothered him if he'd been interested in what they had to say. He loved to talk if one thought led naturally to another and ideas grew into others. But talking to some people was like taking a train trip on a switch engine. You kept jerking back and forth and never got anywhere.

Now and then Matthew wondered if he was some kind of a misfit. Not every one was so choosy about the mental qualities of the girls they took out or married. Other dimensions were all important. But most of the time he considered himself fortunate, mainly because he knew he wanted to teach for the rest of his active life. He dismissed the idea of ever returning to be a college professor before the end of his first semester in Room 147 at Reid High School. There were problems but none that he couldn't handle. He never had to call upon the principal for help in enforcing discipline.

The pattern of his lifework was trimmed to precision by the realization that nothing would ever be more satisfying than enlivening the minds of students. He felt a deep-down sense of being in place when he saw that history was coming alive for some of the girls and boys in his classes. Evidence that they saw the effect of the past on the present and felt the flow of the continuing stream of events inspired him to try to be an even better teacher.

He began to make short trips to other towns in the eastern Indiana counties looking for information about the Delaware and the Miami tribes of Indians. One summer he went south to Corydon, the first state capital, and visited the site of the forts of Old Vincennes.

His interest in local history and the life of the past led him to farm auctions. He began to collect articles others were throwing away or selling for next to nothing. He caught flickers of smiles on the faces of other bidders. He could read their minds. *That young teacher with his head in the clouds don't know any better'n to throw money away on no count trash.*

He couldn't have told anyone why he stored the spinning wheel, two oxen yokes, cherry seeders, and wool carders in the corner of the woodshed. But he found time now and then to rub the wood sections with sandpaper and oil the metal portions.

Sometimes he talked to Lola about moving to another part of town, someplace nearer to school. "We could either sell this place or rent both sides," he said. "I'm making enough to pay on a place."

"It's up to you," Lola said. "I'm contented. But I'd be the same about anywhere, I guess. It's what I do and who's in it that makes a place home. Not the walls and roof and chairs and such."

Matthew read the for sale ads in the newspaper and even looked at a few houses. But the reason for moving wasn't strong, and he somehow couldn't commit himself to a debt. The thought of doing so was a weight in his mind.

Instead he spent some of his savings to attend summer sessions at the normal school in Muncie. It wouldn't do any harm to see if professors over there saw history in the same light. He rented a room in a house on a street called Tally Avenue. The landlady said the rate would be cheaper if he'd share the room with someone else. But Matthew considered the two extra dollars a small amount to pay for the right to decide when he talked and to whom.

Lola went to Ohio for five days and visited her brother the first week Matthew was gone. Then she went out to the old neighborhood and caught up on the news. She had much to tell Matt when the summer quarter was over.

"The Spencer farm has been broken up into five sections. That new owner has an eye for business. Your grandfather's probably storming up there behind the pearly gates."

"Now Lola," Matthew said. "There's no discord in heaven, is there?"

"Then Uncle Spencer's not very happy — in case that's where he landed. Fussing and fuming were meat and drink to him."

Matthew was more interested in what Lola had to say about Garry C. "He's left," Lola said. "Up and joined the Navy. That's what Martha Gail said. She gets postcards with names she can't pronounce. Garry's folks don't live around there anymore. They moved back to Tennessee."

The news that Garry C. had enlisted didn't surprise Matthew. "He always pretended everything was a ship, the stoneboat and the hay wagon and even the workhorses. Sometimes I felt a little seasick listening to him talk about waves and tides."

"Seems surprising," Lola said, "that a boy born and bred out here where there's not even a good-sized lake should have such a hankering."

"Maybe I'm partly responsible," Matthew said. "Garry C. didn't like to read for himself. But he'd

74

listen to anyone who did it for him. The last year we lived on the farm I read *Moby Dick* through twice to him. That was when Papa began taking me with him more."

Lola didn't say much about the four-day visit with her brother and his family. Matthew knew she didn't hit it off with her sister-in-law. He wondered if they'd had a spat or even a quarrel but didn't ask. Lola answered his unspoken question one evening a week after school started. "I can't get Elsie off my mind. She doesn't look well to me. She didn't complain. In fact she didn't have much to say. At the time this seemed like an improvement. But — well it wasn't natural."

When the news of Elsie Allen's death came Matthew had the feeling that Lola was prepared to receive it. But he couldn't understand her mood. She sat and stared out the window, sometimes for as long as half an hour at a time. Usually, at least her hands were busy with patching, crocheting, or knitting.

Does she feel guilty because she and Elsie quarreled? Or isn't she well herself? Sometimes the thought of illness is contagious.

Before winter eased into spring another alteration was made in the pattern of Matthew's life. Lola made up her mind to go to Ohio and live with her brother. She debated and brooded for weeks before deciding and she grumbled about the mental turmoil she was going through. She blamed her sister-in-law for dragging her brother to another state and dying and leaving him among strangers.

Matthew pointed out that Elsie hadn't chosen to

leave her family through death and that Ray Allen had lived away from Indiana for over twenty years. "He couldn't be among strangers."

Lola didn't listen. She didn't even expect an answer. Talking aloud was her way of solving problems and coming to a decision.

When she quit talking and began packing Matthew knew she meant to go and he helped her all he could. He even erased her greatest worry.

"This place is home to me," she said on her last night in the house. "But I can make any place homey. It's you I can't replace. It tears me up to think of you being here alone doing for yourself. I wouldn't want to think I put that clouded look back in your eyes."

"Clouded?"

"Oh, Matthew. You know how lonely you were in the big house — with all your mother's company crowding you out."

"I'm a grown man, Lola."

"I know. But age don't cancel loneliness. Sometimes it's multiplied by the years."

"Well. Let me put your mind at rest," Matthew said. "I'm thinking about changing schools. I don't much like the idea of living here without you to make it into a home."

"Land sakes! Where would you go?"

"I heard of an opening up in Delaware County at a new consolidated school in a little town called Oak Hill."

"That's not too far away from here," Lola said. "You acquainted with anyone up there?"

"Only one," Matthew said. "An English teacher I learned to know in Earlham."

"A girl?"

"No. Not a girl."

Lola left on the first of April and three weeks later' Matthew had been hired to teach in Oak Hill that fall. He walked up and down the streets on his first Saturday afternoon in Oak Hill locating and inspecting the places on the list the township trustee gave him. Four homes in the small town took roomers. Matthew called on all of them and went back to speak for a room in the first house he had checked. It was in the square brick home of Tod Haynes, a widower, on the street back of the general store. "It's chancy maybe," Mr. Haynes said. "Rooming in a place where there's no woman to cook and clean. But my sister lives next door. She takes good care of me and is willing to do the housework for two. When do you want to move your things in?"

"Well, I'd *like* to settle in as soon as school's out in a couple of weeks. But maybe I'd better stay in Richmond where I'm known. I'd be more likely to find work."

"That's no drawback," Mr. Haynes said. "There's work to be done here. I'll put in a word for you here and there. Maybe you could check back in a week or so."

"No maybe about that," Matthew said. "I'll be here a week from today. Early."

9

Matthew lived in the brick house that summer and for six months after school began. Then he and Dora Mattern, the fourth-grade teacher, were married and he moved into her square white home on the south side of Maple Street. He'd seen the dark-haired woman in the post office and general store a few times before the beginning of the school year, but didn't know she was a teacher. No one introduced them until he went to the principal's office to ask if there was a key to unlock the map case.

"You folks met?" Mr. Blodgett said as he swirled his chair and pulled out a lower drawer of the rolltop desk.

Matthew looked directly into the teacher's gray-green eyes. They were as clear as water in an untroubled stream. She didn't wait for the principal to complete the introduction. "I'm Dora Mattern. And you're the new teacher."

"Matthew Kirk."

"I know," she said. "You couldn't be in Oak Hill all summer without being known."

They walked down the half-flight of steps of the first floor and paused as girls and boys streamed past them and parted to go to various classrooms. "You always taught here?" Matthew asked.

"In this town, but not this building as you already know. It's new. And you?"

"I've been at Reed High School in Richmond for nine years."

She's figuring my age, he thought. And for some reason he couldn't explain he added, "I had a hard time getting out of college. Couldn't break away."

"I haven't yet," Miss Mattern said. "I went a year and now I go back every summer."

Matthew's first impressions of Dora never changed. He learned more about her in the next weeks and succeeding years but this added knowledge did not alter the cameo imprint of that first meeting. Her direct and honest eyes, the waved sweep of her hair, and the etched clarity of her speech were facets of the picture in his mind. He felt that she always meant everything she said. She may have been reserved about making comments but she was never affected or devious.

He rarely saw Dora during school hours but they soon fell into a pattern of walking home together. Matthew often stopped at the Mattern house for a few minutes. He replaced a broken hinge on the picket gate to keep it from sagging and dragging. He ran a line of gray putty around the wide window on the east side of the sitting room to stop the rattling caused by the buffeting of wind. He put new rings on the green pitcher pump in the kitchen, when it began to bring up sand from the depths of the well.

It was only natural that Dora fix him a bite to eat on the evenings when his repair work lasted until suppertime. She never made a fuss or acted as if she thought of Matthew in any way different from any other person who happened to be around at mealtime.

Within a month Matthew realized that Dora was the person who could fill a void in his experience, an emptiness so deep that he'd never dared to probe it. And he had the kind of intellectual honesty that forced him to ponder on what role he'd be wanting Dora to play. *She'd never be filling Mama's place,* he thought one December evening. *She couldn't because they're so different and I'd never expect to cut her to fit another's pattern.* Lelitia had been snobbish, primarily concerned with appearances, and in many ways selfish Dora was gentle, friendly, and without pretense.

Sometimes as Dora moved about the kitchen Matthew thought of Martha Gail and Lola Allen. She floured chops and steaks by shaking them in a brown paper bag as one had and cut egg noodles in strips no wider than a blunt pencil lead like the other. But these were only ways of doing things. Dora's nature was unique and he delighted in the continuing discovery of its piquant and refreshing quality.

Matthew began to feel that his relationship with Dora was an anchor. Oak Hill was home to her and so it was the place he wanted to be. He hadn't been in any hurry to start going to church and now he was glad he'd waited. At first he went about the time Sunday school was over and sat at the end of the third pew from the back in the middle section. Oak Hill learned that Miss Dora was going with the new teacher when she came up the basement stairs where she taught a primary class and sat beside Matthew.

After they were married this pattern didn't change. Matthew was asked to take over the class of junior high boys and never was a member of a group of his peers. This suited him fine. He didn't want to expose or declare his views about the Bible or God to people whose ideas might confuse him. "I figure it's up to me to study and ponder on my own," he told Dora, "and not expect others to do my homework. I don't want to get all riled up arguing."

"How about those boys in your class?" Dora asked. "Aren't you giving them some of your views?"

"A few," Matthew said. "But I warn them not to take my word or anyone else's until they've searched the Scripture."

"You think they do?"

"More than before. Since I quit using the quarterly. I can't teach another man's opinion of the Bible. Particularly when I don't agree."

"You may get some criticism for not using the literature."

"Could be. But if someone objects to me teaching straight from the Bible I'll have my own opinion of him. *And* be ready to step out."

Dora was the one who stepped out of a teaching position. The town was surprised and many people were dismayed when she resigned at the end of the year. Matthew had advised her to be sure she wanted to give up teaching. "You may miss it more than you think."

"Possibly," Dora said. "But I'd like to give home-making a try. Maybe I feel this way because I was resigned to being an old maid teacher. How I hate that label."

"Don't know as I blame you," Matthew said. "Like most tags people hang on others, they are either inaccurate or leave out part of the truth, or both."

If anyone in Oak Hill ever thought that Dora hoped to have a family they'd have dismissed the idea as improbable. This opinion was nullified a few months before Susan Melinda Kirk was born. Matthew was uncomfortable about being a father for a long time. He'd never had any experience with babies. He had no preparation for the demands and the intrusions. Always before he'd only been responsible for himself. Marriage to Dora hadn't changed that situation. She was self-sufficient and neither of them had whittled away at the other's mold or violated the other's sense of individuality. At first Dora seemed to accept the minute by minute and hour after hour responsibility of another life without a flitter of disturbance. But Matthew was upset when meals were late and his sleep interrupted. He wasn't jealous. His relationship with Dora was not threatened or altered. It was just that his sense of comfort was ruffled.

The baby was four months old before she became an individual to her father. Dora had left them alone one windy evening. "I want to get up to the store before it closes. I need some No. 50 thread. Or do you want to go?"

"No. No. I'll stay," Matthew said. "Do you good to get out. You'll get cabin fever."

"Well, I'll not be long. If Susan wakes up, which she shouldn't, jiggle the cradle. That usually quiets her."

Wonder how she knows that? Matthew thought

82

as Dora left by the back door. *Surely a four-month-old baby hasn't formed habits.*

Matthew unhooked, then unlaced the brown shoe-strings, and slipped his feet out of the oxblood shoes and wiggled his toes. He edged his high backed rocker to the east window of the sitting room and looked out over the dusk-shadowed yard. The wind skittered dry maple leaves across the brittle grass and plastered them against the pickets of the fence. The bare branches of the cherry tree shook in the strong gusts and quivered when the wind ebbed.

Likely to turn off cold any day now, Matthew thought. *Good thing we got the coal bin filled.*

He heard sounds from the cradle, a kind of squeaky grunt. He rose from the chair and walked to a spot where he could see what the baby was doing. Even in the twilight he could see that her eyes were wide open. He leaned over. Were they changing color? They looked gray like Dora's, not blue as they'd been at first. As he watched, the baby yawned and stretched her arms above her head, keeping her fists closed. *She looks — just like a person,* he thought. And in that instant her identity became clear, distinct, and infinitely precious to him.

If Dora noticed any change in his attitude toward their daughter she never said anything about it. She wasn't given to analyzing. When Matthew offered to give Susan her bottle or get up at night or urged Dora to get out of the house more often she simply accepted the help.

As time went on she let Matthew tell her of discoveries she'd made days or weeks before. When the

baby inched her way off the faded quilt she didn't tell
Matthew she'd put her back four times that day. When
the little girl pulled herself up and stood holding onto
her father's chair, Dora let Matthew think he was
the first to see the move.

As Susan grew and her individuality flowered Matthew began to think that he and Dora were born to
be parents of the wondering child. It had taken them
longer than anyone else in Oak Hill to begin building
a family but perhaps this was an advantage. Sometimes Matthew thought that working with other people's children had given them some idea of bad
parental practices. Listening to students had developed
their intuitive sense and sharpened their instinctive
knowledge of what went on in the mind of a child.

But there was something else, another factor, that
accounted for the fact that Susan Melinda was never
out of place, seldom out of order, and rarely seemed
unhappy. Matthew was able to pinpoint this factor
one morning when the child was between the ages
of two and three. He'd called home from school at
noon. "Susan's cold any better?" he asked.

"Well," Dora said. "I don't know how to answer
that question accurately. She's better. Her cough's
not as tight and raspy. Does that mean the cold's
not faring so well?"

Matthew grinned. He liked Dora's crisp teasing. It
was like eating a pickled beet after two slices of
chocolate cake — an added piquancy.

"She's right here," Dora said. "Wait a minute."

Matthew heard a chair being moved and said,
"Hello, Skiezicks. How's my girl?" When he didn't

get an answer, he said, "It's your Papa, honey. Don't I sound right?"

Dora broke in and said, "She keeps looking in the ear part. I think she's trying to see you in the little holes."

"I have to get to class," Matthew said. "Good-bye, Susan. Your Papa loves you."

He heard a soft and muffled sound. Before he could ask what was happening, Dora said, "Matthew, you should've seen what she did. She put the receiver to her heart and hugged it."

Tears misted Matthew's eyes as he hurried down one half flight across the wide hall and up the full length stairs to his classroom. This was his free period. He needed to grade papers and he did mark a few. But his mind was occupied with comparisons. He was lining up his memories of childhood opposite the circumstances in his present home. It was a contrast of love and loneliness, of companionship and contention of felicity and faithlessness. And for the first time in his life he felt sorry for the child he'd been. He'd never hugged anyone by long distance. Never even thought of it.

Maybe I can do some rectifying, he thought. *Give Susan what I never had, now that I see what I see.*

10

Dora and Matthew never discussed their ideas on the home atmosphere they wished to provide for Susan. Both of them seemed to want to build a protective cocoon for the child. And they rarely disagreed on the matter of discipline. *Actually,* Matthew thought one day when the oval-faced child was six, *there's not been much need.* Then he had to admit that his view was prejudiced.

Susan and her father seemed to vibrate to the same chord, and their natures to be written in a wondering key. Matthew could never take credit for being patient about answering the child's questions. He either knew and wanted to share his knowledge, or was curious and wanted to investigate the same thing.

He always stopped when Susan came to him asking, "What does it mean?" or "Why does it grow that way?" And he never missed an opportunity to guide her into the path of learning. He couldn't always explain the mysteries of nature but he hoped to enhance her awareness of its design. They both waited patiently for the bell-like blossoms of the purple and white morning glory to narrow against the noonday sun. They sat without making sounds that might startle the hovering hummingbirds, whose wings vibrated so rapidly that they could not be seen. "They're like the spokes of the carriage wheels," Susan said. "They aren't there when the horse goes fast."

Matthew had enough intellectual integrity to search his mind to analyze his purpose in adding to Susan's store of knowledge. *Do I want her to outshine everyone when she starts to school? Will my pride be hurt if she's not at the head of her class?* This inner searching was a kind of governor of his conversations with his daughter. He might lead her to the killdeer's open nest in a cornfield, but he let her ask the questions and tried not to say more than she wanted to know.

It was Susan who heard the plaintive cry of the gray-brown bird one summer day. "Is it hurt?" she asked. "It sounds sad."

"That's its nature," Matthew answered. "Let's climb the fence and see if we can catch sight of her, or the nest."

"Won't Mama worry if we're not back? She said be sure to get home so she could wash my hair and dry it in the sunshine."

"We'll make it, honey," Matthew said. "We've come this far and it's not more than a hop, skip, and jump over to the cornfield."

"Are *you* going to hop, skip, and jump?" Susan asked.

"That's just a manner of speaking. What I'll do is walk and leave the livelier ways of traveling up to you."

The stalks of corn were high as Susan's knees and the curling blades whispered and rustled in the summer breeze.

Matthew spied the killdeer's nest before they saw the bird. Four blue eggs speckled in brown lay in a hollowed out place in the mealy soil.

"Are they safe, Papa?" Susan asked. "Won't animals or something bother them?"

"That's another part of this bird's nature. Let's see if we can catch up to the mother. She'll show you how she protects her home."

They followed the "Klee-Kleer" call until they saw the killdeer limping away from them between two rows of growing corn. "Oh, Papa. It's crippled," Susan said. "Its wing must be broken."

"No. That's what I want you to see. Keep walking and watching. They'd gone the distance between ten wooden fence posts when the gray-brown bird soared into the air, circled, and headed directly back toward her nest.

"She was fooling us, wasn't she?" Susan said. "Acting like she was crippled so we'd follow her."

"That's right," Matthew said. "You see, she can fly back to her eggs faster than we could walk, or even skip, or jump."

They crossed between stalks of corn, climbed the woven wire fence, and headed across the pasture field toward Oak Hill. Susan scuffed puffs of dust as she walked in one of the wheel tracks of the gravel road. Matthew took sideways glances at her face and wondered what she was thinking. Was she in some private world where he'd be an intruder? Her brown braids bounced on her shoulders as she walked and beads of moisture glistened on her high forehead. The July Indiana air was heavy with a sweltering steaminess.

"Papa," Susan said as they came within sight of home. "How'd the killdeer know? What told her how to take care of the eggs?"

"Instinct. Pure God-given instinct. That's the only explanation I can give."

After he'd spoken Matthew wondered, *Does she understand the meaning of "instinct"? If she doesn't she'll probably ask. But — I don't know that I can find ways to put that into words.*

After Susan started to school, Matthew tried to avoid questioning her too much about what happened in the classroom every day. He wasn't worried about how she'd get along and he knew Miss Michaels was a fine teacher. He simply wanted to share in Susan's experience. He wanted to be to her all that a father should be and had the feeling that knowing what was going on would enable him to give support when it was needed.

He had one free period during the school day, and always found an excuse for going to the first floor during that time. It didn't take more than a minute to stop at the door of the first-grade room until he caught a glimpse of Susan. Sometimes she was writing in her wide-lined tablet, with her tongue curling at the corner of her mouth, absorbed in her work. Sometimes she was sitting in one of the small red chairs with curved backs, ready for a reading lesson. She was always busy, never staring out the window, resting her head on the desk, or turning to talk to a classmate. Matthew often thought, *I'd like to have a roomfull of pupils like her. But then I'd have to scramble to keep ahead of them.*

As he relished the joy of watching Susan grow and seeing her mind develop, Matthew was often reminded of his father. Had he enjoyed any of his son's childhood? If so, wouldn't he have stayed at home more in spite of the lack of compatibility with his wife?

Susan was eight when Andrew Kirk answered some of Matthew's questions. The two branches of the family didn't get together more than four or five times a year. Andrew was making Mr. Clark's second farm into a paying venture and he was absorbed in this proposition as well as in building up his own stable. He now owned two trotters and three pacers and had made enough money to buy a small plot of ground from Mr. Clark and build his own house, a six-room red brick structure. "I always liked the look and feel of brick," he said. "Both old and new. They've always seemed safe to me and I like the color of them."

Dora and Matthew saw Ellen Newton, Andrew's stepdaughter, almost every week after Susan was born. She married Clyde Endicott, a young farmer who lived east of Oak Hill out toward Springvale. Ellen raised white wyandotte chickens and brought eggs to town every week. Dora was one of her regular customers. Eating at the Kirks on Friday noon soon became a habit with Ellen, except for the days when she had to cook for threshers or haymakers or on days when snow clogged the roads in one direction or another.

Sometimes Matthew slipped home at noon to visit with Ellen and hear what news she brought from New Castle. During one of these brief mealtime visits Ellen said, "I wouldn't be too surprised if your Pa stopped by here sometime later in the day."

"That right?"

"Yes. I had a postcard from Ma asking us for Sunday dinner. She said your father was aiming on going to Muncie to see the carriage maker about a new sulky."

"In case he comes, call me, Dora," Matthew said. "I'll grade papers here instead of at school — no, don't bother. I'll scoot home as soon as the dismissal bell rings whether he's here or not."

Matthew wasn't surprised to see his father on the porch when he came within sight of the house later that afternoon. But he was startled to see the rig at the hitching post. A line from the bridle on Prince, his father's gray pacer, was fastened to the plate-sized iron ring and the silver-maned horse stood between the shafts of an ebony sulky with canary yellow wheels.

Matthew stopped and ran his hand over the tufts of the black leather seat. "Nifty looking outfit," he said.

"The best," his father said. "Or the best Will Bartle had to offer, leastways."

"Ellen said you might stop by. But I didn't figure you'd be driving."

"Why not?" Andrew asked. "It'd have been next to impossible to get that cart home any other way."

"Think you can make it back before dark?"

"Sure, with time to spare. This horse is a fast stepper. I thought I might take you and Susan for a little ride. If you're willing."

It only took fifteen minutes for Prince to pace up and down the four streets of Oak Hill. Susan sat on her father's lap and trusted him to hold her when she leaned sideways to see the whirring wheels, or forward to watch the clicking steps of the horse's iron-shod feet.

"Can you come in for a while?" Matthew asked as they pulled up to a stop.

"No. I'd better head south," Andrew said. "Dora and I had time to confab before school was out."

"Good-bye, Grandpa Andy," Susan said. "And thank you for taking me for a ride." She put a foot down then turned and put her arms affectionately around Andrew's neck.

Matthew watched his father's face. *What is he feeling? Love or regret? Or both?* In that moment, as during so many other times, he felt as if he were outside a scene looking on. He wasn't a part of what he was seeing, only an observer, with a clear view.

Andrew cleared his throat with an imitation of a cough. "Takes me back," he said, "to when you were that age. But it's not a pleasant trip — not because of anything you did — but — "

Matthew didn't know what to say. His father's pain almost impelled him to say, "No matter." But his knowledge of the need for expiation of guilt controlled his impulse to speak.

"In the house, talking to Dora, a lot of things got unraveled," Andrew said. "He leaned over and pulled the long leather whip from the socket on the dashboard. He flicked its whang tip in the air as he talked. "A man's a mixture," he said. "Or maybe it's more accurate to say he lives on two levels — or somewhere in between. Dora made me see that."

"How?"

"Well. It's not easy to say this. But you two have a marriage. She feels cherished and respected. That's as plain as the nose on my face."

"I hope so," Matthew said.

"I have the same thing now with Inez. But — with your mother and I it was a contest of wills in lots of ways. Two selfish people trying to use each other. What held us or brought us together — it wasn't the stuff of which homes are made. Not the kind children deserve. Not like little Susan has."

Matthew wished that he was six or eight again so that he could impulsively demonstrate his feelings as Susan had done a few moments before. He'd never felt this depth of communication with his father before.

"I reckon this is hard for you to understand," Andrew said.

"No sir!" Matthew said. "I know what you're saying, as well as what you've not said. I could tell you that's all water under the bridge, and it is, except in what we remember. The past is hurting you now. I see that."

"Only as it affected you."

"But I survived. Without any noticeable scars. So be glad for how things are now — for all of us."

"I am. I am. But I can't help wondering. What brought you through the trouble? A lonely kid with two selfish parents."

"I've thought about that now and then, mainly when I see misery in other children's faces. I think it's in some people's nature to rise above such things. But I had help. Martha Gail and Lola. And you were often there when it counted."

"Sometimes, maybe," Andrew said. "But not often. Not enough. Well. That's said and I'd better roll along. You folks come out."

"We will."

Matthew stood at the gate and watched until the sulky, the horse, and the driver were out of sight. *I must tell Dora about this conversation,* he thought.

He heard the screen door bang and turned to see Susan coming toward him with a book in her hand. "Want to hear me read, Papa?" she asked. "I didn't miss one single word today."

They sat down in the slatted porch swing and Matthew braced one foot so the words wouldn't sway in front of Susan's eyes. He listened with part of his mind but he wanted to gather the little girl in his arms, to circle her in a protective embrace. *How can people give someone the love they've never had?* he thought. Then the answer came in a kind of instinctive knowing. *Such love is not a human quality. It's a heavenly gift.*

11

With few exceptions Dora and Matthew were able to shelter Susan from attitudes which would frighten or distress her. Sometimes they wondered if they were too protective. "You know how it is with hothouse plants," Matthew often said. "They get used to warmth and shelter and can't stand the shock of the cold world."

"I don't know as she's bundled that tight in cotton," Dora said the day before Susan's thirteenth birthday. "She does go to public school. And she doesn't have her nose in a book all the time she's home."

"I know that," Matthew said. "But she moves in a world apart even at school. She doesn't take up with all the notions other girls get like sewing beads all over the front of their dresses."

"Mothers do the sewing," Dora said. She sat down at the kitchen table to add to her grocery list. All the Kirks, and Ellen and Clyde, were coming for dinner on Sunday for Susan's birthday. She scratched her head, beneath the coronet of braids, with the rubber-tipped end of the red pencil. "I thought of having chicken," she said. "But that'd be no treat for Ellen and Clyde. Beef would be better. I think I'll get a nice big roast."

Matthew made no comment. He knew that none was expected. Dora solved problems during her one-sided conversations. He sometimes wondered if she dealt aloud with her quandries when she was alone. He went on with what he was doing, attaching a shelf to the sill of the south kitchen window. Dora wanted a place for her geraniums, where they'd get the sunlight and she'd be able to enjoy their rosy color and spicy fragrance.

"I'll get a nice big roast," Dora said as she added to her list. "Now that that's settled I'll get on with the baking."

"Where's Susan now?" Matthew asked as he pried a lid from a can of white enamel. "It's past time for her to come home from her music lesson."

"She asked permission to stop by and see Lillian Conner's new dress. They probably got to talking."

"It's almost dark," Matthew said. "And she ought not to be walking home alone."

"Oh, lands sakes! Who in this town would hurt that child?" Dora asked.

"Well no one that I know of at the moment. But you've got to allow for the unexpected."

"Why borrow trouble?" Dora asked.

The change in the life of the Kirk family came on a summer afternoon five years later when Susan's eighteenth birthday was a few months away. Dora was alone that morning and no one ever knew exactly what happened. Matthew was working at the schoolhouse sandpapering and varnishing the desks which had been scarred by gouges of knife blades and pin tracings. He felt he'd erased the attempts to insure immortality when initials and names disappeared by the abrasions of sandpaper.

Susan was enrolled in the summer session at the teachers' college in Muncie, and wouldn't be back in Oak Hill until the 4:20 interurban stopped at the end of the street on its way to New Castle. Matthew strolled home, taking time to see what early summer rains and summer sunshine were doing to Oak Hill. The grass in yards had changed from the yellow green of early spring to a deep shade of emerald. Tight clusters of rosebuds embroidered the vines of the rambler on Mrs. McShirley's picket fence. He knew the buds would soon be pink tufts.

He started up the front porch steps when a patch of blue caught his eye. His heart lurched as he rounded the porch and saw Dora. She was lying on the grass under the cherry tree. He didn't see any movement, not then nor after he stooped to touch her face.

Life as he'd known it stopped for Matthew when he realized that Dora had ceased breathing. He picked her up, not noticing that the fall had broken her neck or that ivory cherry seeds clung to her chambray dress. Matthew lived in an alien world the next days, weeks, and months. He couldn't bear reality. Dora had given life meaning. She had soothed the memory of his lonely childhood, the insecurity he felt after the death of his mother and the change of schools. She had brought him contentment and a sense of security etched in love.

Now a cloud descended on Matthew. Everything was gray. Nothing seemed natural and normal except Susan, and even his view of her was partially veiled by the mists of despondency.

He forced himself to go to school when September came, but his heart was no longer in teaching. He knew he couldn't go on as though nothing had happened. He submitted his resignation to the principal effective in the spring. He didn't want Susan to drop out of college and stay at home with him, but couldn't arouse himself from his gloom enough to make a forceful protest.

He sat in the armchair with the tilt back most of his waking hours. Most mornings he was sitting upright in front of the base burner when Susan came downstairs. He never moved the brass rod, which supported the padded back, to a lower notch. The upright position was indicative of his rigidity — his braced posture against misfortune. He rarely bothered to pour nuggets of hard coal into the heating stove. He sat staring into the glowing coals not seeming to notice when the fiery fingers of flame died down to a glow. He'd shake his head and say, "You oughtn't to be lifting such heavy loads," when Susan picked up the wide-mouthed bucket of fuel. But he didn't move, didn't even throw the blue and white coverlet away from his legs.

Sometimes Ellen Endicott came in and tried to "jolly him out of the dumps." She'd tell him what was going on out at the farm or bring him news from New Castle. She tried scolding, attempting to get him on his feet, but her words didn't seem to reach Matthew. He rarely smiled and almost never answered — just stared into the gold and coral coals.

His only moves were toward Susan. He always patted her hand when she brought his food to his chair on a black tray. Sometimes tears misted his blue eyes as he watched her run the carpet sweeper or wipe coatings of Bon Ami from windows. He answered all her questions and responded to most of her remarks, but not in sentences — only in words or phrases. He saw no wonder, felt no joy, and was never moved by curiosity. He held onto reality only by the slender thread of his love for Susan.

But that thread was strong. It held him back from the pit of complete mental darkness until he could make faltering moves toward the point of being reconciled to living without Dora. The first giant step came on a late winter evening when freezing rain was beginning to silver-plate Delaware County. An east wind blew sleet particles against the windowpanes. Susan shook down the ashes and added a whole bucket of coal to the firebox. "I'm going to fix your supper now, Papa. And I think I'll eat in here — with you. The kitchen's a little chilly around the edges."

Matthew turned and looked out the window after she left the room. Darkness would come early that night. The air was smoky gray. He looked across the room and had an impulse to get up and light the china shaded lamp. He hadn't wanted to see its glow for months. He told Susan that its milk white light hurt his eyes. The truth was that he was reminded of Dora's pleasure when he brought the lamp home from the Banner furniture store. She loved the spray of roses which circled the edge of the domed shade.

"Here's your favorite supper, Papa," Susan said as she walked carefully to his chair. "I think I've finally learned to poach eggs."

Matthew nodded as he looked at the squares of buttered toast and the eggs which were coated in peppered milky opal.

"Looks tasty," Matthew said. "And things *have* been tasting better lately."

"Maybe that's because I'm finally learning how to cook."

Matthew didn't pat her hand this time. Instead he reached up and ran one forefinger down her flushed cheek. "You do fine. Say, honey. Before you go to get your tray, would you mind lighting that lamp? To brighten the room."

Susan leaned over and rested a cheek on the top of his head. Neither spoke. Their hearts were full and their minds were meeting. There was no need for speech.

Susan pulled the footstool up to the side of the stove. "My legs are too long now for me to be comfortable on this," she said. "But I've always loved it. It's a favorite of mine."

"Your Grandma made it."

'I know — of empty cans and layers of carpet," Susan said. "Mama told me."

The room was warm and the lamplight reached beyond where they sat. They didn't talk as they ate but there was a sense of communication. A broken line was mending.

Susan walked to the window before she took the trays to the kitchen. The outside world was a somber place now, all shadows and shades of gunmetal gray. As she watched, a car crawled down the slippery street and eased to a stop. "That's Aunt Ellie," she said. "Why in the world would she come to town on a night like this?"

The mainspring of Matthew's life was rewound in the coming days and weeks. The functioning had faltered and sputtered but within twenty-four hours he'd resolved to put his name on the substitute teacher list and was back in the classroom on a regular basis before the end of the month.

As spring approached Matthew began to realize that he'd emerged from one trial and was facing another. Susan had met Arthur Dirksen Garland at church the night Ellie came to town to urge the girl to get out of the house. Within a few days the square-shouldered young man whose hair was the color of sun-bronzed wheat came to the house and rang the doorbell. It was the first of many calls.

Ellen Endicott moved to Oak Hill before the winter was over. Her husband's heart hadn't withstood the pneumonia which set in after a spell of the grippe. Ellie meant to stay on the farm but a late snowstorm had isolated her for three days and she followed the snowplow to town.

Susan and Matthew convinced her that there was room for her in the square white house and in their lives. The thought that people might talk if they knew Ellen wasn't his real sister flitted through Matthew's mind. But he shooed it away. *There's always someone who's ready to make gossip out of an innocent fact. Always has been and always will be.*

For a while Matthew kept hoping Susan would go back to school. Ellen was there to take over the housework. But Dirk's influence increased and there was no sign that Susan intended to reenter college. Matthew thought of discussing with Ellen how he felt about Dirk, and asking her to see if she could convince Susan to see less of him, or even question the wisdom of their friendship. But somehow these moves seemed disloyal.

He even considered going over to Springvale and doing a little cautious investigating.

He'd heard of the Garland family but people talked more about the Dirksens. They had the money and the land. After Dirk began coming to the house Matthew often wished he'd paid more attention to what people said about Bertha Garland. He'd heard that she controlled the money and spoiled her son. No one mentioned her husband.

After Matthew realized that Susan was seriously interested in Dirk he questioned his own curiosity about the Garlands. *Is it because my instincts are warning me about that boy? Or would I feel the same toward anyone who might want to marry her?*

Susan did not surprise her father when she told him she and Dirk planned to marry early in the summer and move into the tenant house a mile away from the Dirksen home place. He'd seen the handwriting on the wall and steeled himself to accept its meaning.

He didn't like Dirk. There was a look in his eyes that made Matthew want to order him out of the house. "He's cold and selfish and — surely that's a sensual mouth."

The father in Matthew wanted to interfere and try to prevent the marriage. But something in his nature deterred him from doing anything to cancel another's right of self-determination. His inner wrestling and mental anguish were painful. Sometimes he thought that he'd never have survived if he hadn't recovered from his breakdown before Susan met Dirk.

He often thought of his own childhood and the incompatibility in the marriage of his parents. Was history going to repeat itself? Did he forsee unhappiness for Susan? Or was he a jealous, possessive father. Still he spoke to no one of his doubts, not even to Ellie.

Matthew schooled himself to rely on Susan's judgment. He knew she was young and innocent but she had the ability to rise above pettiness. "But she doesn't realize what kind of life may lie ahead for her."

Matthew didn't go to the Springvale parsonage for the ceremony. Susan didn't ask him to attend and he knew that neither of Dirk's parents were to be there. He was relieved that he wasn't expected to witness the rite which marked Susan's move to another way of life.

He made plans to fill that day with activity. He went to school as usual and he and Ellie drove over to New Castle and stayed all night. He tried desperately to keep his mind from wandering in the direction of Springvale.

12

For several months Matthew was almost stoical in his attitude toward Susan's marriage. It had happened. It was a fact. He felt that she'd never be happy, at least not for long, living in the framework of the Dirksen-Garland attitudes toward life. He also faced the fact that he was disappointed, and not just because Susan hadn't gone on to college. There was a sharper pang in his mind. His image of Susan was not that of a girl who'd make an ill-considered marriage. Or did he really know her? Was there something in her nature that responded to Dirk's insistence? Something he didn't want to see? He often asked himself, "Did I expect her to stay in childhood?"

He shied away from going over to the shabby farmhouse. Dirk had never been cordial and his manner became more defensive after the marriage. He spoke to Matthew but never initiated conversations. He responded to Matthew's father-in-law questions and comments either in short terse sentences or not at all.

Matthew knew that Susan was uncomfortable because of Dirk's coldness toward him. He caught glimpses of the veiled look in her gray-green eyes and noticed a slight quivering of her lower lip. Her nature, or his view of it, was indelibly printed in his mind.

But he could not go without seeing her and was sure she'd not want him to stay away. So he formed a pattern of visiting her. He soon realized that Dirk would not be in the house except for meals and not always then, unless the weather was bad. Even then he worked at the big farm most of the day.

Matthew sometimes left Oak Hill right after school and visited until five or a little later. He usually managed to think of some small treat for Susan, a book, a magazine, a jar of Ellie's red currant jelly, or a chunk of sweet chocolate.

He wanted to do much more. It was soon apparent that Dirk was tightfisted about money — and probably other things. Susan had always run her left shoe over at the heel. After a few months Matthew began to wonder how she kept one brown oxford on her foot. "How about letting me take that shoe into Muncie and getting a rebuild job?" he said one late September evening. "Before it's too late."

"Well, I *am* walking on my uppers," Susan said. "But I don't know what I'd wear around the house. I hate to take either pair of my good shoes for everyday. They're still nice."

She was standing at the end of the kitchen table dipping golden applesauce into glass jars. One leg of the table was shorter than the others, or perhaps the floor slanted at that corner. The steaming jar kept sliding and Susan's tongue curled on her lower lip as she concentrated on keeping the scalding pulp from dripping on her hand.

Matthew turned his head. The look on Susan's face

stabbed him. *She's not happy I can tell. How bad is it?* Could he bear to face what his instincts were telling him? At that moment, on that dry and sultry evening, he realized the painful truth. His daughter was an unloved wife. He'd sensed from the beginning that Dirk was either incapable of cherishing a woman or did not know the definition of love. And a relationship which did not include tenderness would damage Susan as long as it lasted. It would violate her.

Matthew's thoughts were in a turmoil as he drove back to Oak Hill. He couldn't have told anyone what he'd said to Susan before he left except that he suggested that she be ready to go to town early on Saturday morning. "We'll see about getting you shod."

She hadn't dissented. Tears came in her eyes as she rubbed a cheek on his shoulder. "It'll be nice to get away," she said. "Thank you, Papa."

"No need for thanks."

He ate very little supper that night and hardly noticed the difference between the spareribs, browned potatoes, and custard pie. The freshly ground nutmeg didn't even register on his taste buds.

A breeze came up from the west by lamp-lighting time. The window screens rattled in their setting and the tendrils of the wisteria vine whished against the meshed wire.

"I know I shouldn't," Ellen said, "but I'm going to help myself to another wedge of pie. Want to follow suit?"

"No. Not this time. I'm not as hungry as usual."

"I noticed. Something's heavy on your mind, isn't it?"

"Yes," Matthew admitted. He ran the palm of his right hand back and forth over the top of his head. The movement smoothed the few strands of white hair, then ruffled them again. "Susan."

"I thought so," Ellen said. "You look the way I feel every time I see her these days."

"How's that?"

"Distressed, angry — and a few other things."

"That says it," Matthew said. "Ellie, Susan's marriage was and is and always will be a mistake."

"Possibly," Ellen said. "It's tearing Susan up inside now — that's easy to observe. But I reckon none of us can see far enough into the future to be sure that things won't work out in time."

"I don't see much hope," Matthew said. "And the worst part, besides her pain, is that I foresaw how it would be and didn't lift a finger to stop her."

"I've wondered if you said anything to her. Or if you saw what I saw."

"And what was that?"

"Nothing that's easy to put into words. Just a feeling that Susan Melinda might have been the first girl that Dirk couldn't get without marriage. But that he'd never treat her much better than the other kind."

Matthew shoved the chair back so hard it screeched on the linoleum. He walked to the back door and looked out into the shadowed yard. For some reason he thought of the word "Gethsemane." He stood there in his own private agony and tried to analyze his state of mind. It was another of those times when he seemed to have a vantage point where he could see a scene in which he was a participant.

107

He turned, sat down on a kitchen chair, and talked for over an hour. In that time the breeze became a gusty wind and a heavy shower rode on its pulsing strength. Ellie sat and listened, except for the few minutes it took her to close the windows.

Matthew's mind was purged of pent-up feelings during those sixty minutes. He admitted that he'd refrained from expressing doubts about Dirk because he felt guilty. "If I'd been stronger — kept a grip on myself after Dora's death — this might not have happened. That was a bad time for Susan, a dark and lonely winter."

"I know," Ellen said. "But you can look at that picture from another angle. I've wondered. Did Susan get married to get away from the same thing that caused your breakdown? From living in this house without her mother."

"I reckon that should make me feel better," Matthew said. "But looks like I should have been able to make things bearable."

"In normal circumstances maybe," Ellen said. "But you were both suffering. And give yourself credit. You fought back."

"I'd rather have protected Susan. The pain I felt last summer was for myself. This time — this is a different kind of Gethsemane."

Ellen flicked a strand of hair back from her forehead before she answered. "You don't often refer to the Bible."

"Not aloud. I get suspicious when people sprinkle their conversation with pepperings of Scripture. Lots of times their talk and their actions don't jibe."

"The night of agony that Jesus endured was kind of

108

like our trials, wasn't it?" Ellie said. "And He wasn't suffering just for Himself either. Even if He did have plenty of reason for self-pity."

"You thought I was wallowing in that, didn't you? I remember the night you came in and sent Susan and me off to church. You sort of raked me over the coals — lightly anyhow!"

"That brings up the subject of *my* private feelings of guilt," Ellie said. "That's when Susan got acquainted with Dirk. If I'd stayed home and minded my own business our girl might be in college now — might be a sight happier."

"There's no way of knowing that," Matthew said. "I doubt if we could have kept a girl like Susan hidden. Who knows. Dirk may have had his eye on her for a long time — had her spotted as a future conquest."

Matthew left the kitchen and tried to focus his mind on grading a sheaf of history tests. But Susan's face kept coming between him and the listed causes of the war between the states. *It's time to quit feeling guilty,* he thought. *What can I do now to help and to heal?* A strong resolve salved some of the ache in his thoughts. *I'll try to act in wisdom, not in anger at Dirk or regret over what might have been. I'll be all I can to that girl without adding to her strain or pain. Who else knows her well enough to realize what she needs that I can provide? Or loves her more? And the first thing I have to figure out is how to get her a pair of shoes so Dirk won't know or object.*

The means of filling the need came within two days. The minister's son came to Matthew's door that evening

109

asking if Susan had any college textbooks for sale, "Yes, a few," Matthew said. "She wanted to keep her literature book but the others are upstairs." Even at half price, the books were worth nearly six dollars. *Susan will have enough to buy a good pair of shoes and some left over — a little change to jingle in her pocket.*

Ellie went to Springvale with Matthew on Saturday. Susan was ready and waiting. But she wanted her aunt to see the foods she'd canned. "I have more applesauce than anything," she said. "*Because* I have more apples. And before I forget! I picked up a bag of windfalls for you. The wind blew them down but the grass is thick and they're hardly bruised."

"Well, thank you," Ellie said. "We'll have us some apple dumplings and a pie or two."

"I have another kind of windfall for you, Skiezicks," Matthew said. He told her about the sale of books as he handed the envelope to her.

"That's wonderful," Susan said. "But didn't you buy the books?"

"Nope. Don't you remember? I paid fees and you sold wild blackberries for book money."

"How could I forget? I had scratches from the brambles that didn't heal for weeks, even through two pairs of Mama's stocking legs. Lillian and I suffered a lot for that money. But it was fun."

Matthew let the ladies go to the department stores and the five-and-dime without him. "I'll meet you back at Ballard's Hardware store in a couple of hours," he said. "Then if you've emptied your purses I'll treat you to a sundae at Terhunes."

He went to Penzels and bought a half dozen Golden

Rod tablets. He'd learned that a certain type student used lack of paper as an excuse for not doing lessons. Keeping tablets on hand punched holes in such alibis. He looked around for a gift for Susan, for some little trinket which would bring the light of pleasure to her eyes. And as usual he decided to buy a book. Then he hesitated. He'd noticed that Susan had moved the books she'd taken from home to a shelf in the far corner of the living room. Did Dirk object to reading? Did he become angry when he saw the volumes lined up on the library table in the middle of the room?

I'll slip her some of the new books from the school library, Matthew thought, *and buy her something that won't stand out like a sore thumb.* He left the bookstore and went to a women's clothing store. He bought a heavy rose sweater without looking around more than a few minutes. He felt out of place among all the displays of women's clothing. *Besides this sweater will come in handy. That old farmhouse must have drafts coming from all directions.*

He had a half an hour to visit with others who made Ballards their meeting place. He leaned on the coal radiator which was not yet heated by hissing steam. Three men were loafing on the other side of the front door. Matthew didn't know them and he watched passersby until he heard the name Bertha Dirksen. His neck felt warm and he ran a finger under the stretched collar. He wanted to hear but was afraid to listen.

"She'll never let go of a dollar willing like," one man said. "She squeezes every one till the eagle squawks."

"How about that boy of hers? Isn't she freehanded with him either?"

111

"Some. But she aims to keep him in line. Handing out when that's what it takes. Holding back other times."

Matthew saw Susan and Ellen crossing Walnut Street and hurried out to meet them. He not only didn't want Susan to overhear what was being said in the hardware store, he also wanted to keep her from knowing the Garlands were the subject of gossip. *She always felt bad when little girls said unkind things about her or each other.*

They sat on the wire-backed chairs in the ice-cream parlor and talked as they ate pineapple and strawberry sundaes. Susan showed her father the black oxfords she'd bought and the flowered percale. "Aunt Ellie's going to make it up for me."

"It sort of matches what's in here." Matthew said as he gave her the sweater. "The flowers are about the same shade." They stopped at Jones Sisters' bakery and came out with two coffee cakes and a dozen sticks of candy in three flavors — clove, lemon, and cinamon. Susan loved the thin sticks of spun sugar not only for the flavor but for the lovely colors — garnet yellow and topaz.

"It's been such a wonderful morning," Susan said as they turned onto the Springvale road. I wish — "

"Wish what?" Matt asked.

"That I could go home with you."

"You can. Any time," Matthew said.

"I know. I know what you mean, Papa. If I thought Dirk would be gone all night I would."

"All night?" Ellie asked.

"He takes his mother places to see her folks.

112

Sometimes they don't get back."

"Is he gone now?"

"Yes. To Celina."

"Do you want to go to Oak Hill now?" Matthew asked.

Susan nodded. "For the afternoon anyway. But it'll be best if I'm back before Dirk comes home."

"No problem," Matthew said. "This taxi is at your service, ma'am."

13

The temperature fell twenty degrees that night. Matthew had helped Susan cover her tomato plants and lima bean vines with layers of newspapers and a strip of water stained canvas before he headed back toward Oak Hill. He turned around in the graveled barnyard and glanced toward the house. Susan was standing at the back door hugging herself against the chill wind. She waved and turned. Matthew wished he'd gone in and lit a lamp or two. *She never liked walking into darkness.*

White frost whiskered the world during the night. Every strand of the woven wire fence was edged in silver-white and the grass was coated in snowlike crystals.

"Looks like winter's set in," Matthew said as he brought the Muncie *Sunday Star* in from the front porch. The lightly rolled cylinder showed tracings of frost as if the news of the world was etched by nature.

"Can't be sure of that," Ellen Endicott said. "We often have a spell of Indian summer sometime in October."

"Your crystal ball must be a lot clearer than mine."

"What do you mean?"

"When you look into the future you don't foresee the worst. Even have some hopes for Susan's happiness."

"Some," Ellie said. "But I'm not as good about seeing the now and the past as you are. Sometimes I think you've got a grandstand seat. Or a place like the judges of horse races sit at the Delaware County Fairgrounds. You can see both ways or all around."

"But not too far beyond," Matthew said. "What's on your mind? What's puzzling you about the present?"

"Not the present," Ellie said as she filled the gray granite teakettle from the gushing stream from the pitcher pump. "It's the past that's muddling my mind."

She went on to say that she'd often wondered why Matthew's father and mother didn't get along, what caused the split. "Andrew and Mama hit it off so well which inclines me toward the notion that it was your Mama's fault. And that's unfair of me."

"It's hard to say. My father talked to me some. But I always felt like he was holding back some things."

"People do. To protect themselves or someone. And another thing. You were an only child. So is Susan. Would things have been different if there'd been others?"

"I might have been less lonely," Matthew said. "But I doubt if anything else would have changed." He picked the newspaper up from the hot-air register. The furnace heat had melted the frost and dried out the moisture, leaving the gray newsprint blotchy.

"In Susan's case — I doubt if she was ever lonely. And our marriage, Dora's and mine, was never shaky. Of course, having someone here after her mother died might have kept Susan from reaching out."

"Human life and people-type relationships are a mystery and a puzzle," Ellie said.

"But not the divine," Matthew said. "It's all in a piece. Oneness."

"Matthew Kirk. You amaze me sometimes."

"That's where we're alike. I amaze myself now and then."

Ellen had been invited to eat Sunday dinner with her husband's relatives east of New Burlington. Her brother-in-law came to get her after church. She told Matthew that he'd be welcome but he said mixing too many varieties of kinfolk was like adding red pepper to apple dumplings. "They don't blend. Neither has a good flavor. Not that I ever tried it. The thought sets my teeth on edge."

Matthew was a little restless after Ellie left. He ate the chicken pot pie and stewed peaches his stepsister left, and wandered through the yard and garden to see what damage the frost had done. The leaves of most annual plants were already turning black. Even the sun of Indian summer weather would not revive them.

He thought of driving over to Richmond, maybe going through the park or looking up friends. *But that's a jaunt for a full day.* He went in and put on his corduroy vest and his brown felt hat. He liked to stroll around Oak Hill, stopping when he took a notion, seeing what there was to see. He could have written regular reports on what needed repairing, what improvements were being made, and who was away for a while.

No one was sitting on the slatted benches in front of the post office at the general store. Not even the drugstore was open. There'd be a two-hour stretch after four o'clock when people could buy what they needed or thought they had to have. A half dozen boys were throwing basketballs at a wooden hoop on the school playground. The thump of the inflated sphere and the clang as it hit the rusty hoop echoed in the clear cool air. Matthew began to think he was the only adult in Oak Hill who was astir on that Sunday afternoon. He admitted that the term "sleepy little town" would accurately describe the place at this particular hour. *But most of the time there's more bustle.*

He ambled in the direction of the grain elevator. A section gang was working on the Norfolk and Western track. He'd always wondered what a railroad repairman's life was like. Some of the crew might be in sight. *I could strike up a conversation and learn something today.*

As it turned out he was not to enhance his knowledge of the business of railroading that day. As he rounded the corner he saw a man coming toward him. *That's Joe Hinshaw,* he thought. Joe had been hired to teach science at Oak Hill school that fall and Matthew hadn't had time to get acquainted with the slender man whose shoulders were sometimes hunched. Someone said the new teacher was bothered by asthma — or was it hay fever?

"Good afternoon, Mr. Kirk," Joe said when Matthew came within hearing distance of the end of the brick walk.

"Matthew's the name I like to hear from adults. I get Mr. Kirked enough at school." The two teachers

117

talked for nearly ten minutes. They discussed the art of laying bricks at a diagonal to make the zigzag pattern on which they stood. They made brief comments on the coming election. School people were cautious about voicing opinions on the selection of local officials. They discussed the unrest in Europe and Matthew said he reckoned the world might be in for another futile war.

"Futile?" Mr. Hinshaw said.

"That's how it seems to me. Nothing's settled until the fighting stops. Then agreements are worked out. It'd save waste of lives and materials if the agreement came beforehand."

"Isn't that a little idealistic?"

"It is. But I wouldn't want to live in a world without ideals. Maybe that's because of my background. I went to a Quaker college."

Joe began to shiver. "I'd better go inside. I have this breathing problem. That's why we left Indianapolis. We thought teaching in a smaller school might be less strenuous." He asked Matthew to go inside and meet his wife.

"I wouldn't want to spoil any plans."

"You won't. Nancy's working on a course she's taking. May not even notice we're around."

Nancy Hinshaw came to the long sitting room, was introduced, and asked to be excused after a few minutes. Matthew judged this couple to be five or six years younger than he was. Nancy was slender and straight but her dark red hair was etched in gray at the temples.

The afternoon eased into dusk before Joe and Matthew

ended their conversation. Nancy came to the door and said, "We'd like for you to stay and eat a bite with us, Mr. Kirk."

"No. No. My sister will be home anytime if she's not already. She's likely wearing a path to the window looking for me to come wandering home."

He and Joe Hinshaw became good friends that winter as well as foils for each other's views. "That man whets my mind," Matthew told Ellie one cold March evening. "I can't agree with his views which seem atheistic to me. But I have to sharpen up my own thinking in order to disagree with him to my own satisfaction."

"Do you think he listens?"

"He listens. But I doubt if I've changed him one iota. Most arguments aren't for mind changing — just opinion fixing."

Winter seemed to have tightened its grip on Oak Hill and there was no sign that it would give place to spring. The heaviest snowfall of the winter had come two days before. A moist curtain of big flakes descended through the air blotting out the sun and limiting visibility. Five inches accumulated in 6 1/2 hours and then an east wind swirled the deposit into road blocks and travel hazards.

School was dismissed at eleven o'clock on Tuesday and had not convened until Friday morning. Hiatt's Hill at the south end of town became a sled-packed slope. And the general store ran out of bakery bread a whole day before deliveries could be made from either Muncie or New Castle. Star Route 3 was closed in both directions. Matthew said he could smell bread baking whenever a door opened. He'd been to the post office soon after the mail train chugged in from the north.

"Wonder how Susan's getting along — out there all by herself," he said as he unbuckled his felt-top artics.

Ellie was hunched over the Wheeler and Wilson sewing machine guiding trimmed pieces of flowered percale under the presser foot. The treadle squeaked a little as she rocked it back and forth.

When the two sections of Susan's dress were seamed into one, Ellen turned and looked at Matthew over the top of her gold-rimmed glasses. "This time next year, and before that even, she'll not be alone."

Matthew realized what Ellie was saying. No need to hedge. He'd anticipated hearing that Susan was pregnant sooner or later and wouldn't have been surprised to hear it some time ago. He'd prepared — or was it steeled — himself for this eventuality. Just as he'd been uncomfortable about playing a father's role, so was he reluctant to assume the part of a grandparent. He assured himself that this feeling didn't come from a dread of becoming old. He'd decided that the spirit never aged and that the years wouldn't burden him if he parted with some of the baggage of human pleasures and pains now and then.

His concern was for Susan. A child could be another trap keeping her bound to Dirk. Matthew knew that she'd love a child in the way every new inhabitant of the world deserved. *But she's vulnerable. And she'll suffer for her children's pain as I do for her.*

Ellie was watching his face when he brought his attention back from the inner sanctum of his thoughts.

120

"It won't be easy for her," Matthew said.

"No. It's not now. But we've got to find ways to help. Any way at all."

"Like you're doing now? Making that dress?"

Ellie nodded as she tied the threads at the end of the seam.

At the time of the March snow Susan's baby was due in seven months. He didn't dare let himself think that she'd need a doctor during these days when roads were drift filled. But he'd like to know she was all right. He wished he'd blundered on with the impulse to pay to have a telephone installed in the farmhouse. *What would she do if she did need help? Dirk's gone so much.*

Purplish shadows of evening were creeping across the drifts when the telephone rang. Ellie was in the kitchen sifting yellow cornmeal into salted boiling water. This kind of weather called for mush, cold milk, and brown sugar.

Matthew answered the ring and heard a man say, "Is this Susan's pa?"

"Yes — " Matthew's throat tightened.

"Well, I'm Seth Garland. I made it across this field a while ago. Susan wanted me to let you folks know she's fine. She reckoned you'd be fretting."

"We are," Matthew said. "You sure she's all right? Doesn't need anything?"

"She's fixed good," Seth said. "I uncovered the woodpile and about filled the back porch and I stopped by the grocery for some cheese and bread. In case Dirk don't get back."

"He's gone?"

"Yep. He and his ma are stranded somewheres."

"I hate to think of Susan being alone."

"That's part of what I have to say. I'm aiming to trudge back that way. Or hitch a horse to the stone sled. Some may say I oughtn't to leave this place untended. But in my mind people come first. So you folks rest easy."

"I appreciate this, Mr. Garland," Matthew said. "It's fine of you to call."

Matthew put the receiver on the hook and walked toward the kitchen.

"We're not the only ones that want to look out after Susan. That was Dirk's father. I'm going to make a point of getting acquainted with that fellow. Find out whether he stays in the background out of choice or because of compulsion."

"Could be a little of both," Ellie said.

"Maybe. But one reason's probably stronger than the other. What tips the scales? That's what I'd like to know."

14

Matthew did find several opportunities to speak with the slender quiet man who seemed to be an appendage to the Garland family. Susan had once said that her father-in-law had nothing to say about how the farm was managed. "He works all the time but Bertha is the boss — of Dirk too."

"And you?" Matthew added. "Does she tell you where to step and when?"

"She tries," Susan said. "Mostly she tells me what not to do — like waste time reading. I guess it's a good thing I don't see her much — or else there'd be sparks."

Matthew hadn't fed this conversation with questions or comments. He could see that Susan was on guard, probably afraid she'd say more than she should — afraid she might worry him.

In the months before Mary Anne Garland was born Matthew had three opportunities to get acquainted with Dirk's father. The first came on Sunday after a pale sun and the county snowplow had cleared the roads. "I don't like running the risk of running into Dirk," he told Ellie. "I might up and speak my piece about him leaving Susan alone during the blizzard. But I'd like to be sure she's not in need — is in good shape."

"Well," Ellie said. "If you're going I'll tag along. Two of us ought to be able to smooth over the rough places, or the bare spots, in the conversation. Besides I can mark the hem in Susan's dress and leave it for her to whipstitch."

Ellen packed half of an old-fashioned cream pie and a bouquet of her dried strawflowers into a basket. Susan met them at the back door. "I hoped you'd come. But didn't really expect you."

"You here by your lonesome?" Ellen asked.

"Except for Dirk's father. He's out at the barn putting clean straw in the calf stall. He mentioned that Bertha called the veterinary for a couple of the beef cattle. So Dirk took off."

Matthew wandered out to the barn. "No use to shed my boots then put them on again. And Mr. Garland might be gone soon."

He opened one of the double doors and the acrid ammonia odor of the animal-trodden bedding stung his nostrils. He walked through the chaff-coated feeding room until he saw Dirk's father in the light of the back door. He was lifting manure-matted straw into a low wagon with a four-pronged pitchfork.

"Howdy," Seth said when he caught a glimpse of the visitor. He leaned the tool against the side of the door and walked toward Matthew. "Come over to cheer Susan up, I reckon."

"If that's what she needs, we'll try."

"The way I see it," Seth said, "some folks need people more than others. Some need things."

"How about you, sir?" Matthew asked.

124

"I reckon I'm an oddity. I can get along without either to some degree. I get my satisfieds out of taking care of things. Like these here steers. And growing things and such as that."

"Well, I thank you for taking care of Susan," Matthew said. "It took a load off my mind when you called."

"No need for thanks. I wouldn't want any harm to come to that girl. And seems like she's the only human being around that has any need of my caretaking."

Matthew had another conversation with Seth in early June. Ellie and Susan were hemming squares of cloth for what Matthew called baby britches. "I could have done it by machine," Ellie said. "But that makes a stiff seam. Might be scratchy."

The sky was as blue as the pitcher someone brought Dora from the world's fair in St. Louis. Fluffed cotton clouds eased across the azure dome. A heavy rain had made the grass soggy and the fields too wet for cultivating. Dirk was away with his mother. Susan didn't say where — if she knew.

Matthew followed the line of woven wire fence that ran back to the woods. He noticed the curled petals of purple violets in the aisle of thick grass which edged the field. A small brown toad leaped out of hiding and bounced across the cigar-colored soil. Crickets squeaked from somewhere in the tall timothy. Then Matthew heard the plaintive call of a killdeer. He'd often stood in wonder at the gray-brown plover's instinct-guided existence. There was no other way to account for the mother bird's protective moves. There couldn't be enough intelligence in the bird's brain

125

to lead her to pretend to be crippled when molesters neared her nest. She had no books to tell her that the species *man* would follow her if she dragged her wing on the ground as if it had been broken.

The sound and then the sight of the killdeer brought a question to Matthew's mind over which he'd often pondered. How much better would the quality of our lives be if we let the instincts and intuitions given to us by God direct more of our moves?

He followed the mother bird until she suddenly soared into the air and circled back toward the four eggs in her hollowed out nest in the soil.

The resounding blows of an ax came to him as he neared the back fence row. He focused until he saw a blue chambray shirt in a clump of white birch sprouts.

"Grubbing I see," Matthew said when he was within hearing distance.

"None too soon," Seth Garland replied as he blotted his forehead with an old bandanna. "These shoots grow fast. But I feel ripped in two about chopping them down."

"How so?"

"I like clean fence rows," Seth said. "But the sight of a full grown birch is as pretty a sight as I'd ever hope to see. There are no doubt plenty of spots in the world which'd be bettered if one was to be set out."

"True," Matthew said. "I have one in the backyard. The silver bark pleases *my* eye too — or my mind."

The two men talked casually letting one subject hook on to the next, as the tendrils of a wild grapevine reach out in the growth process. As Matthew headed back toward the house he thought *that man knows more about nature's ways than anyone I know — or than anyone around here realizes.*

The meetings with Dirk's father kindled Matthew's curiosity, not that it needed much fanning or fuel. His sense of wonder about life and people led him to speculation. He had to guard against being inquisitive or as Dora and Ellie put it, "plain nibby." In the case of Seth it was a mystery to Matthew how and why he'd ever married Bertha Dirksen. And it was just as puzzling to try to figure out why Dirk's rich, materialistic mother had chosen gentle Seth. He remembered Martha Gail's explanation of why people married one another. " 'There's no accounting for taste,' the old lady said as she kissed the cow."

But Matthew didn't think taste was a factor in most matings. *In fact a lot of folks don't even know each other very well until the knot's tied. Then their differing tastes begin to show up.*

Matthew gained a sunburst of insight into the Dirksen-Garland relationship when he met Rhoda Collins in the Oak Hill general store one day. Her face looked familiar but he couldn't give it a name. This bothered him until she spoke. "You're Mr. Kirk, aren't you?"

"I am," Matthew said. "The only one around this town — as far as I know."

"Well, you don't know me," the bright-eyed lady said. "I'm Rhoda Collins. I live in a notch in the Dirksen land."

"You mean on the back road?"

"Yes. Behind your daughter."

"You know Susan?"

"No. And I don't feel quite comfortable about not calling on her. But — well it might not be any help for her to be sociable with me."

"Want to talk about this?" Matthew asked. "I've got a bumblebee's nest of questions buzzing around in this head of mine."'

Mrs. Collins looked around. "Maybe we'd better go outside." She picked up the brown sack of groceries and Matthew carried the oil can and the length of black stovepipe. They stood on the root-humped sidewalk and talked for no more than ten minutes. But as Matthew walked up Maple Street he felt that he'd heard a capsuled history of the Dirksen family which included much of the story of the Springvale neighborhood.

Ellen was at an all-day meeting of the women of the church, so Matthew ate alone. He spooned the chicken salad his sister had left onto salty soda crackers and ate three helpings of the first peas from the garden. Pieces of the jumbled puzzle assumed order in his mind. Rhoda's summary cleared up the mystery of the mismatching of Dirk's parents. Bertha wouldn't have married anyone who would have sought an equal place in the family affairs or might have tried to dominate. Seth loved working on the land and was ready to move away from the restricting influence of a father who told him every move to make and then criticized him for not having any initiative.

The Dirksens, Bertha and her father before her, had one purpose in life, to own more land than anyone in Eminence Township, Rhoda had said. "And they do. That's why they don't have any use for me. Our

128

forty acres is surrounded by their fields. They wanted to buy it and we wouldn't sell."

Rhoda hadn't mentioned Dirk's name, but she'd made one oblique reference to him. "Bertha uses money as a club to keep folks in line. Seth ducks."

Matthew wondered as he poured a third glass of lemonade, *What does Mr. Garland do for money? Is he paid for his work?* Then he shook his head. *I'm never content with what I hear. I always want to go deeper, know more. But that's natural. There are always hidden reasons and unknown factors.*

He went out to the garden and reset twenty-seven cabbage plants. He gently pulled them from the cluster which had grown from seeds so as not to damage the hairlike roots. Then he spaced them a foot apart in a shallow trench. As he worked he wondered what people around Springvale thought of Seth Garland. *Do they call him mealymouthed for letting Bertha run things? Or is he a sponger to them, trying to get hold of some Dirksen money? Does anyone see that the quiet gentle man has a kind of inner strength which doesn't need the support of land or money? Anyone besides Rhoda Collins?*

Matthew was ready to leave for school one morning in early October when someone knocked at the front door. He buttoned the coat of his blue serge suit as he walked through the sitting room. He was both surprised and alarmed when he saw Dirk's father. How did he get here? Was something wrong — with Susan?

"Morning," Seth said. "I got only a minute. I rode in with a neighbor. Susan's near her time. And getting the corn in is all fired important. I may be out of

129

place — but she'd be better off here."

"She having pains?"

"No. No. Not that yet. But I figure it won't be long."

"Then I'll go get her. Now. Want to ride out?"

"I might as well. Joe's picking up stuff at the hardware store. It takes him awhile. He has to mix buying with chewing the rag — more talking than business."

Matthew stopped at school to tell the principal he'd be an hour or so late. It took that long to get Susan back to Oak Hill. She was eager to get home. She left a note for Dirk and shook her head when her father offered to stop by the cornfield. "No. He's probably way back somewhere. And you're in a hurry to get back to school."

Susan was at her father's home for four days before the ordeal of childbirth began. Dirk had come in on the second evening to see if she was all right. He was ill at ease but Matthew thought he showed some genuine concern. Dirk asked Susan if she wanted him to stay and even gave her a five-dollar bill "for extras."

"You can go on back," Susan said. "Nothing's going on here. Nothing for you to do. And there's lots to do there."

"Sure is," Dirk said. "Looks likely we'll have a bumper crop of corn. Ma's trying to find someone to put up a crib in a hurry."

How about a crib for the baby? Matthew wondered. *Don't the Garlands plan for the young one to have a place to lay its head?* He resolved to go to Muncie the next day and buy a baby bed.

He left early Saturday morning with a list so long that he didn't get back to Oak Hill until nearly three o'clock.

130

Susan's pains had begun at ten o'clock and within twelve hours Ellie was using the safety pins and Vaseline Matthew had brought from town. And the small ivory bed was assembled in time to cradle Mary Anne Garland.

Dirk wasn't on hand when his daughter was born. No one answered the Garland's telephone when Ellen had tried to call. "I could go out there," Matthew said, "but I don't want to leave."

"Don't," Ellen said. "You're needed here. For my sake as well as Susan's."

15

Matthew's anguish over Susan's apparent unhappiness eased somewhat a few months after the birth of his first grandchild. At first he was more worried than before. She had the same look on her face as he'd seen on her mother for a few weeks after Susan was born. He remembered the day he came home from school and found his wife and daughter crying, one in gaspy wails and the other in silent sobs.

He wondered who was in pain. Dora was huddled in the big rocker, with a faded and worn quilt pulled up to her chin. The baby was on a pillow in the deep-seated rocker. Dora pushed the chair with one foot, up down, up down. But she stared out the window with tears overflowing and running down her reddened cheeks.

"What's wrong? With which one?" Matthew asked.

"Me," Dora said. "Oh, Matthew, I don't know what's the matter with me. Nothing looks right. The world's gray."

"Well, that's nothing to scare you. The sun's down."

"No. That's not it. It's been this way all day."

Matthew was frightened. The panic in his wife's eyes gave him a feeling of chilliness. She wasn't always sunny natured. She was irritated sometimes and often puzzled. But these moods were facets of her personality. It was as if her nature was veiled in strangeness. He didn't know what to say or do. So he looked around the shadowed room and said, "I reckon we need a little light on the subject." He lit two lamps then went to the kitchen to see if he could scare up some dinner. He took four eggs and a dish of stewed tomatoes out of the icebox.

He was adding a few nuggets of Yellow Jacket coal to the embers in the range when Dora came to the kitchen. "Here let me take over. You'd better change your clothes."

"But if you're feeling — "

"Puny?" Dora said. "That fits. But I've felt this way for two weeks or so."

"I didn't notice," Matthew said.

"I didn't aim for you to find out," Dora said. "I was ashamed."

"Ashamed?"

"You go on and change. I'll tell you while we eat. If Susan Melinda lets us."

Matthew was puzzled. *How'd I live around so many women and not know what was bothering Dora?* Had his mother and Martha Gail and Lola Allen ever had such moods? Had they hidden them? Why?

Dora had turned an omelet out on a sizzling plate when Matthew came downstairs. Links of country sausage were browning in the skillet. Tea was steaming in the thick ironstone cups.

Dora steered the conversation away from herself

133

until she'd spooned canned cling peaches into gold-banded dessert dishes. Then she told Matthew that Ellie had stopped by as usual with the three dozen eggs. She bought the baby a dress she'd made, white dimity with blue ribbon run through the edging. Dora also reported that the new minister had called asking if they wanted the baby baptized. "I told him we'd decided to wait until she was old enough to have some say so in the matter."

"You've talked and talked, beating around the bush. Now what's wrong that you're ashamed of?"

"Maybe ashamed is only a part of how I've been feeling. Scared is more like it."

"Scared of what?"

Dora looked directly at him. Her lower lip quivered. "Of losing my mind," she whispered.

Matthew reached across the table and folded his fingers over her clenched fist. "You? Why — "

"Well. A lot of women talk about this. How they feel blue after their babies are born. How things seem dark and different."

"What did Dr. Bell tell you about listening to such talk?"

"I know what he said. That women magnify and dramatize to make men suffer. Because their part of having children is painless. But he's a *man*."

"That's true. But he did go to school. He's learned about such things."

"From who?" Dora asked. "From men. Not from personal experience."

Matthew scratched his temple with one forefinger. What could he say? How could he reason logically

134

with his wife who was talking illogically?

Dora got up and poured herself another cup of tea. "That hits the spot. Nothing's tasted right lately. I didn't notice. What kind of tea did you get this time?"

"Same as usual."

Dora went on tiptoe into the sitting room. "Sound asleep," she said. "I guess she got tired of crying. And so am I. You know, Matthew, I'm not sure I was having the childbirth blues as bad as I thought. Oh, I've not been myself. But right now it seems like it was partly because of what I'd been told."

"The power of suggestion you mean?" Matthew said. "In that case I suggest you do your own thinking."

He didn't speak to Ellie of seeing the same signs of depression in Susan. She told *him* the evening after Dirk had brought his wife and daughter to Oak Hill for a brief visit.

That evening Ellie sat down in a rocker and began to talk. Matthew listened without putting down the newspaper until he heard the words, "After I told her that her mother pulled herself out of the same dark mood she began to pick up."

"How'd you know about Dora?"

"Oh, Matt. I came in town at least once a week. And Dora and I were good friends. I saw how she looked, and she told me how she felt. Not that I didn't know."

"How? You — "

"Didn't have any children. No. But I was old enough to realize how bad Mama felt when the twins were born. And women talk."

"No doubt," Matthew said. "No doubt about that."

Except for his concern for Susan, Matthew was satisfied and content with the pace of his own life. His days moved in a measured rhythm. He taught school for eight months, worked on repairing and refinishing classroom furniture during the summers, and made short trips around the state now and then. The more he learned about Indiana history the more he was convinced that he'd only scraped the surface. And a sense of regret grew stronger in his mind. Many stories would never be told. No one was around who knew the truth firsthand. Lively imaginations and poor memories either exaggerated or clouded the facts. He never stooped to pick up an Indian arrowhead without wondering who had been in its target. But it was too much to expect that a Miami or Delaware would return from some hunting foray and prepare a diary of his day. Matthew visited country cemeteries sometimes, climbing rusted iron fences and pushing matted tangles of vines aside in order to read inscriptions. He wasn't interested in the geneology of his own family. He knew enough about his antecedents to satisfy that twinge of curiosity. He was looking for traces of the state's history, for names of men who'd either helped or hindered the carving of Indiana from the Northwest Territory.

He was never away from Oak Hill for more than one night and rarely missed a weekly visit to Springvale. Susan didn't get home often, so he kept in touch by spacing his visits at regular intervals and at times when he'd not come face-to-face with Dirk.

On these evening or Saturday morning trips Matthew saw that Susan's children were her solace and her comfort. *Is it the gentle love she feels for them or the dearness of their natures which is alleviating her distress?* He liked the word alleviate. It eased his mind.

He saw Susan's strength of character ripen. She never whined. She rarely mentioned Dirk's name but neither did she complain. Instead of being martyr-like because of the lack of money and hinting that she needed cash, she assumed the job of caring for a flock of chickens.

"I'm still scared to reach into a nest," she told Matthew. "When I hunt eggs I carry a stick and hold their heads down so they can't peck me."

"Do they lay pretty well?"

"I don't really know what well is," Susan said. "I didn't take *chickens* in college. But they help. I bought paint to brighten the floor around this rug last week. And hard-soled shoes for Neal. And even had a little left for jingling."

Neal, Susan's second child, was a serious little boy. As Ellie put it, he seemed to take to his grandpa Matt from the very first. He'd sit on Matthew's knees in contentment for as long as an hour at a time. And the day Matthew delivered the little red wagon, Neal ran and clasped his arms around Matthew's knees. *He's like Susan,* Matthew thought. *His feeling shines on his face. It doesn't take words to know what's going on inside them.*

Aside from his short jaunts and the visits to Springvale Matthew did little socializing after an unbroken race horse dragged his father to his death on an Ohio dirt track. Ellie still went out to visit her mother regularly but Inez' other children were married and Matthew felt that neither mother nor daughter needed a third party in their sessions of mutual consoling. Ellie still grieved for Clyde and probably always would. "He was all I had or needed. Or ever will," she'd said more than once.

There was one home in Oak Hill where Matthew as a widower didn't feel out of place. It had become a custom for him to eat Friday evening supper with Joe and Nancy Hinshaw. The two Oak Hill teachers drew duty as ticket takers at the same home games of the basketball teams. In winter they ate soon after dusk and hurried to open the double doors and let people in out of the cold. In summer they ate in the fading light of long afternoons and either played croquet or sat on the front porch. Wherever they were, at whatever time, they talked. Nancy rarely made comments. This began to bother Matthew. *Maybe she's tired of me hanging around. Could be jealous maybe.*

He told her what he'd been thinking when he met her on the walk outside the post office one morning. She'd stepped aside to let two rope-skippers pass. Matthew saw a wistful look on Nancy's face as she watched the little girls bounce away from her.

He stopped to talk and was both startled and puzzled when tears misted her eyes after he spoke of what was on his mind. "No. Matthew. Don't think such a thing. And don't quit coming."

Then she looked at him and bit her lower lip before going on. "I have to trust you. Or share my burden. Joe's not well. Never will be. And he's not going to be with me much longer."

"Does he know?"

"Not because he's been told," Nancy said. "But I'm sure he's aware. And it seems to help him to go on as if he didn't. Your visits and even the arguments rouse him more than anything he does. He — sits and stares — too much — far too much. I hate to leave him alone for very long."

NANCY HAD been a widow for nearly a year when Matthew heard from Ellie that Susan's fourth child was on the way. He'd kept on going to the Hinshaws for a while but not on a regular basis, just to take down window screens and fix leaky faucets. He began to see that he was following a path he'd trod once before when he repaired gates and pitcher pumps for Dora. And the idea of marrying Nancy some day began to seem like a possibility, one he liked to consider. *Of course there's Ellie to think of. She's made a good home for me. And Susan. Now more than ever I feel sure she'll leave Dirk sooner or later, for one reason or another.*"

Once in a while Matthew felt a little restless, especially during the hours between the dismissal of school and bedtime and on Sunday afternoon. The longer he lived the more convinced he became that life was meant to be progression not stagnation. He sat on the porch one early spring evening and took a kind of personal inventory.

This April day was as warm as late May. It was like an advertisement for what was to come. Matthew knew that there'd be some bad weather ahead. Cold rains and wind and even the possibility of snow. He remembered the year when the deep clusters of the purple lilacs, the golden sprays on the forsythia vines, and the fuchsia tracings on the red bud tree were tufted with glistening snow. It was a lovely sight, but somehow unnatural.

Matthew watched a plume of smoke curling from the chuffing engine of a Norfolk and Western train. It separated into puffs as it rose into the turquoise sky, and the setting sun tinged it in lavendar. *They're like smoke signals from an unseen Engineer,* Matthew thought. *All such sights are of His design, I guess.*

He leaned back in the porch rocker and for the first time faced the fact that he wouldn't be teaching school for the rest of his life. *Provided my days go on for that long, what can I do with myself?* He considered several possibilities and the idea of rocking until the end of his time wasn't included. *What have I learned that I can use? Which of the tools of living are sharpest?*

He knew that this was a matter which would require much meditation. He'd mull it over in his mind and surely in five or six years he'd come up with an answer. *And I might come up with more ideas than I'll ever have time to put into practice. Which would be good — in a way.*

16

Life for Matthew moved in an even flow for several weeks. Then it churned in a whirlpool of change. Two telephone calls were the forerunners of major adjustments. The first one came from Ellen's sister, Ann. She told Ellen that their brother was sick and alone. "Mama went over there but she's really not strong enough to take care of him. And I'm pretty tied down with things here."

Ellen turned from the telephone and tapped the toe of her brown oxford on the rug before telling Matthew the side of the conversation he hadn't heard. "My duty's clear," she said. "I'm needed there — now."

Something in her tone of voice implied an unspoken meaning.

"Now?"

"Yes, Matthew. I've seen how the land lies. In Nancy Hinshaw's direction. And I wouldn't want to be a block in your path."

"You wouldn't. This place — you're welcome — no, that's not how it is. I don't need to say you're welcome to stay. Like I was granting you a favor, This is your home."

"But two women under the same roof," Ellen said. "You know what they always say."

"Well that speculation's a little premature. Nothing's been said about either Nancy or I changing our place of residence."

"You will sooner or later. And it could be that God is taking a hand — guiding me to a place where I could do some good."

"You mean *another* place," Matthew said. "I guess I've never told you how grateful — "

"Then don't," Ellen said. "Keeping house for you and Susan and the little ones has kept me going. It's been my reason for living."

"Won't you miss Oak Hill? The church and your friends."

"Certainly," Ellen said. "But I figure they have churches over in Ohio. And good people."

She told Matthew that she'd been debating for some time about moving out to the farm to take care of her mother. "I know she likes to be independent. But there may be other ways to take care of her. John's house has nine rooms. We could divide it so each of us could have our own kitchen and privacy. But that's a little premature, as you put it."

Ellen left the next Sunday after scrubbing, dusting, and scouring the house for nearly three days. She used one morning to cook ahead for Matthew. He told her she had so many pies, cakes, and cookies stashed around that he'd have to have a bake sale. And he did stop by Springvale on the way back from Ohio to leave one deep-dish apple pie and two dozen oatmeal cookies with Susan. It wasn't easy for him to keep the basket hidden from Ellie but he didn't want to hurt her feelings.

Susan and the children were sitting in the shade of the two maple trees at the north side of the house when Matthew drove in the lane.

"I thought Aunt Ellie might ask you to bring her past here," Susan said. "To say good-bye."

"That was her intention until we climbed in the car. Then she began to cry. Said she couldn't stand one more good-bye. That her roots were being mangled and needed time to mend."

"Poor Aunt Ellie. She probably feels she doesn't belong anyplace."

A soft breeze stirred the leaves of the tree, and sparrows twittered in the wild grapevines on the wind-mill tower. "I don't think that's true," Matthew said. "It seems to me Ellie's torn because she feels she's a part of so many places."

"That's not the way it is with me," Susan said. "I've never felt at home, except in one place."

Matthew tried to mask his concern. What was she trying to tell him? Had the time come to speak with her about the state of her marriage? He watched Susan's face. She'd never looked more beautiful to him in spite of the faint purplish shadows under her eyes.

The children came back from the car carrying the basket and asking for permission to eat some of Auntie's cookies. Susan looked at her father and shook her head. He didn't hear whatever she might have been ready to say. Not that day.

Ellen's leaving did clear the way for Nancy and Matthew to talk of marriage and begin to make plans.

There was never a particular moment when they came to an agreement to marry. That became an assumption. They spent more time discussing where they'd live. The Hinshaws had started to buy the house in the middle of the first block off Maple on Walnut. They'd made some improvements but Nancy could see more that ought to be done.

Matthew said that this would probably always be true even if a person planned and built a new house. After he made that statement they added the possibility of building to their list of alternatives. It was at this time that Matthew talked to Nancy about Susan's marriage. He was sure that she'd been aware that there was incompatibility. She couldn't help but notice that Susan and the children always came to Oak Hill without Dirk.

"I'd like to keep the house available," Matthew said. "In case she ever decides to use it as a refuge. And something tells me she will."

"There's no reason why you can't plan for her," Nancy said. "In fact it'd be simpler. Both of us have fully furnished houses. We couldn't possibly put everything into one. And Susan might have need of her mother's things.

"I couldn't sell them," Matthew said. "And I don't think Dirk would take to the idea of getting Kirk-used furniture."

Matthew didn't take Nancy to Springvale but neither did he avoid speaking of her to Susan. A few opportunities came for the two women to get better acquainted on Susan's visits to Oak Hill. There were a few times when she could use the truck, days when Dirk and his mother went to buy cattle or visit Bertha's relatives.

One of the times came two weeks after Ellen left. Susan was in Oak Hill by nine o'clock on Saturday morning. "I came to clean and cook," she said as Matthew met them at the gate.

"Don't you have enough of that to do?"

"Well, I guess so. But it's more fun here. And I promised the children we'd have a picnic. Like we used to do. Back along the bend in the creek. Why don't you ask Nancy?"

"Well, if it's all right with you."

"It's fine with me."

Matthew took the baby, Little Ellen, with him when he went to issue the invitation. "Your mother can get more done if you're with me," he said. Neal and Mary Anne decided to go along at the last minute. They'd had to debate the question of which was more fun, going uptown, as they called a walk around Oak Hill, or looking at the stereopticon pictures, or playing on the two-seated lawn swing in the backyard.

Mary Anne stayed at Nancy's until it was time to walk south and cross the pasture field to join the others for the picnic beside the meandering stream. Matthew had brought the old baby carriage down from the attic and it held Ellen, a stone jug of lemonade, and a folded quilt.

Mary Anne wanted to wade as soon as they settled on a picnic spot on the sloping bank. "I think we'd better eat first," Susan said. "It's past noon. And I for one am starved."

Matthew squinted at the sky. "It's time to be

145

hungry. The sun's started on its downward curve."

Nancy had brought bananas which were a special treat for the children and made ham salad sandwiches. Susan's butterscotch cookies were still warm and the deviled eggs were moist and mounded.

After the meal Matthew leaned on the trunk of a tall walnut tree and watched the older children wade and splash in the clear and shallow stream. The baby was asleep and the sound of Nancy and Susan's soft voices blended with the rippling water as it ran over rocks in the creek bed.

This is the pinnacle of contentment, Matthew thought. He pulled his felt hat down so that it partly shaded his eyes and he let himself edge into a state between sleep and wakefulness. He was in a place where all was pleasant.

Neal roused him by saying, "Look grandpa. I found a shell. See!"

Matthew blinked and took the unhinged half of a bivalve. "This is only part of a shell, Neal," he said. "See. This is where another section was fastened. It opened and shut like a purse."

"Wonder where the other half is?"

"It's hard to tell," Matthew said. "This creek branches off from White River and it's a tributary of a larger stream."

Neal took the shell back to the water saying that he wanted to wash away the mud and the sand so the silver and the pink and the blue of the lining would show better. Matthew moved down for a sitting share of the folded quilt.

"I remember how this creek seemed to me,"

146

Susan said. "When I was the age of Neal and Mary Anne it was as wide as a river. Of course I didn't see a river very often. And never waded in one."

"I know what you mean," Nancy said. "There was a hill on my grandfather's farm. It was a mountain in my mind — until I really saw mountains."

They left the grassy bank at three o'clock. Nancy was choir director at church and a practice was scheduled for five o'clock. Susan didn't seem in any hurry to head back toward the farm. She fixed what she called a bite of supper, leftovers from the picnic plus a skillet of crusty fried potatoes. She was scouring the kitchen sink when Matthew said. "I almost forgot. Your Aunt Ellie left a box of things for you. Up in her room."

"What kind of things?"

"She didn't say. You're to take what you want, or can use, and I'm to find ways to dispose of the rest."

"I'll run up and look," Susan said. "Then I'd better start back."

She never says "start home," Matthew thought.

Susan came downstairs empty-handed except for two sheets. "Is that all you're going to take?" Matthew asked. "Do I have to do something with everything else in that big box?"

"This is what I need most now," Susan said. "Is it all right if I leave the rest — for a little while anyway?"

"Naturally," Matthew said. "They aren't in my way. I've not been in that room since Ellie left. By the way, have you heard from her?"

"Yes. I had a long letter. Maybe I should have brought it for you to read, Papa. But she told me some things that set me to thinking. And I'm not quite ready to talk about what's going on up here in my head. Do you understand?"

"Maybe. A little. And it's all right, Susan. I'm ready to listen when you're ready to talk."

Susan nodded and smiled through mistiness. "I know. You always have been. She walked to her father, and rested a cheek on his shoulder. "Hug me a minute. I need your strength. Or what you give me."

Matthew carried little Ellen to the truck. And he kissed the older children before they climbed to the seat. "I had a good time, Grandpa," Neal said.

"We always do when we come here," Mary Anne added.

"We always *do*," Susan echoed before she turned the key and the motor sputtered into a roar.

Matthew walked back into the empty house, looked around, and felt forlorn. *It's a good thing Nancy and I planned to go into New Castle. Otherwise, I'd sit down and have a good case of feeling sorry for myself.* He pulled his gold watch out of his vest pocket and started toward the back door. Before he turned the brass key he caught a glimpse of the baby carriage on the walk. *I might as well stow it in the attic. Hard telling when Susan will come home again.*

17

Summer had made eastern Indiana a place of flowering and ripening, when the ring of a telephone heralded another change in Matthew's life. He'd oiled the lawn mower that morning and the clacking blades had clipped the grass in both the front and back yards. Nancy walked the 2 1/2 blocks bringing him a quart jar of cold tea and two thick corned beef sandwiches for dinner. "I can't stay," she said.

"I know. You're going to the trustee's office. Sure you want to change jobs?"

"I'm sure," Nancy said. "Mainly because of the time. I'm on the road at least an hour on good days. And when there's snow and ice, Center School seems to be a lot farther away."

They'd already discussed the question of whether or not Nancy would go on teaching. Matthew had asked her what she wanted to do. "Actually, I have mixed feelings. I've wanted to try full-time home-making for a long time. Or I thought I did. But Joe's doctor bills were so high. And maybe I'd be restless with too much time on my hands. So — "

"So you're going to whittle an hour from your working day."

"True," Nancy said. "But it won't be easy to leave Perry Township. It's been a good experience. Mostly."

Matthew didn't ask her to explain what she meant by mostly. He was a teacher. He knew the problems and the frustrations. He hadn't escaped having a few disagreements with principals and other teachers. He often wished he could have kindled brighter sparks of enthusiasm for the whole process of learning in more students.

Matthew meant to go back to the schoolhouse and work that afternoon. He'd varnished himself into a corner in a sense and had to wait for the floor of the front hall to dry before he could work in the elementary grades classrooms. He wandered from one odd job to another, cutting dead sections from the cluster of the rambler rose vine, pulling weeds from the two rows of bush limas, and edging grass away from both sides of the front walk.

He pulled out his watch. *Two-thirty. Later than I thought. But I could still get a row of desks shellacked before evening.* He was drying his hands on the blue-bordered linen towel when the telephone rang. It could be Nancy with news of getting a job — or being turned down.

Instead he heard Seth Garland's voice. "I been down to the other place," Dirk's father said. "Susan says to tell you to come over if you want overnight company."

"Anything wrong?"

"No. But the folks are away. And she figures this'd be a good time to pay you a visit."

"Well. I'll crank up my struggle buggy and start to

Springvale. Were you going to go back — with a message?"

"No. There's no need. Susan seemed to figure you'd come."

"She figured right," Matthew said.

He hurried over to tell Nancy where he was going and stayed a few minutes to hear the news that she'd be teaching fourth grade in the fall.

"Want to ride out with me?" Matthew asked.

"I do and I don't," Nancy said. "I'm about to bubble over with ideas and maybe plans. But I have this feeling. It's not easy to explain something which seems mystical to me. But somehow this visit of Susan's is going to change things for all of us. Mainly for her and for the better."

"It's time. Long past time."

The older children came running out of the house a few minutes after Matthew drove up the graveled lane. He'd begun dusting the car's fenders with a red bandanna. "We're about ready to go, Grandpa," Mary Anne said as she ran across the yard. "Mama's dressing Ellen. She'll be out in a minute."

They arrived in Oak Hill in time for Susan to cook supper and wash dishes before dark. Neal and Mary Anne caught fireflies and played wood tag while Susan sat in the porch swing and her father rocked in his cane backed chair.

The fragrance of mock orange blossoms permeated the evening. Neither Susan nor her father spoke until after the chimes in the bell tower of the church marked the hour of nine.

Matthew rocked forward and tapped his fingers

151

against the porch railing as he spoke of what he'd seen for years.

He told Susan that he and Nancy were thinking of getting married before fall and hurried to add that the house, her home, would be empty and waiting in case she wanted to bring the little ones back to Oak Hill.

"Not three little ones, Papa," Susan said. "There'll be four before Christmas."

"There's room."

Matthew was relieved that Susan neither pretended that her marriage was good nor protested that she didn't want to be a burden to him. *She's ready to make a move,* he thought. *Nancy's instincts were correct.*

There were painful moments during the conversation. Matthew knew that Susan was speaking with tears streaming down her face although she sat in a shadowed corner. "Don't you want to leave Dirk?"

It took a couple of minutes for Susan to manage to speak in a composed voice. Then she simply said that she had to leave in order to survive — in order to protect her children.

Matthew felt a renewed sense of peace that night. His family, as it was now, was under his roof. He knew that Susan might have a bad time when she confronted Dirk with the news that she was coming back to her father's house. *I wonder when she'll make her move,* he thought as he locked the back door and climbed the stairs.

He was surprised as well as relieved when Susan took his car and the baby and went to Springvale the

152

next day. "I'll bring back what we have that we'll need," she said. "If that's all right with you, Papa."

"There's never been a time when it wasn't."

Matthew never saw signs Neal and Mary Anne were disturbed or even puzzled by the move. Circumstances made Susan's explanation believable. "Grandma Garland's sick and your father has to take her far away to a hospital. So Grandpa Matt's going to take care of us while he's away."

Susan spoke only once of Dirk's reaction to her leaving. "He surprised me," she said. "He *said* he didn't want me to go. Of course his mother's illness was preying on his mind. Things are sort of falling apart for him, I guess."

"Do you regret coming home?"

"Oh no, Papa. I feel so much better. More rested. But there's more. I couldn't go on — making all the concessions for the sake of peace. Sometimes I felt like a person who kept on bending backward, farther and farther. I was losing my sense of balance."

Matthew and Nancy were married the last week in August. By that time Susan and the children were settled in the white house on Maple Street. A poultry buyer had hauled away the flock of chickens and Susan had money to buy school clothes. Matthew and Nancy persuaded her to accept help until the baby was born and she could decide what she wanted to do. "Dirk may want a divorce and will have to support the children."

"But that's not what I want. Not *have to* help," Susan said. "But I'm not really worried. I'm sure there'll be a way — without the Dirksen money."

Dirk came to Oak Hill the Sunday after he brought his mother back from the clinic. Matthew was on the porch rocking the baby while Nancy and Susan washed the dinner dishes. He saw the big car coming and wished they'd gone for a drive instead of waiting until after the baby's nap. *But I can't hide Susan and the children. And it's not my right to do so.*

Dirk looked older, thinner. He didn't swagger as he walked. He worked at the knot in his black tie as he came through the gate and up the walk. Matthew looked down. Ellen was asleep. The plump hand rested on her grandfather's arm, fingers uncurled.

"Sound asleep, I see," Dirk said.

"Finally gave up," Matthew said. "Have a chair."

"Susan inside? And the kids?"

"Susan is. Neal and Mary Anne are over on the school playground."

"They all right?"

"Fine. Fine. How's your mother?"

"No better," Dirk said. "And won't be."

"I gathered as much," Matthew said. "From what Susan said you wrote."

"They couldn't do much. And it won't help for long."

Dirk dug one heel into the straw porch rug and rocked with a jerky motion. He stared straight ahead over the porch railing, keeping his eyes on something in the distance, on some spot beyond the yard, across the street and the vacant lots.

Matthew didn't move from the swaying swing but his mind assumed the overall viewpoint which enabled him to see in a circle beyond this time, around the scene and back to now. It suddenly occurred to him that

154

he and his son-in-law had a similar background. Both Letitia and Bertha inherited and controlled most of the money. Only Bertha held on to hers. Both fathers had stayed in the background. But Andrew had finally run away. *Then why didn't Letitia mould me as Dirk's mother shaped him?* All these questions and others circled in Matthew's mind. *Am I a man who feels a cherishing love because of Lola and Martha Gail? Or was Plato right when he said men were born of different metals?*

When Nancy followed Susan through the screen door Matthew looked at his daughter's face. She seemed to read the unspoken question, "Want us to leave?" She shook her head and sat down on the top step, leaving the seat beside her father for Nancy.

She said hello to Dirk, asked about his mother, and then didn't seem able to think of anything else to say. Dirk pulled three envelopes from the pocket of his white shirt saying, "These are for you. Pa says to tell you he'll try to get into town. He misses you — too."

"We'll be glad to see him," Susan said.

"Well it's time for me to head back. Pa can't manage Ma when the pain's worst." He got up and said, "Is it okay if I walk up the street and see if I can catch sight of the kids?"

"Certainly," Susan said.

Dirk turned, leaned over, and ran one forefinger across the palm of Ellen's hand. The baby's fingers curled into a grip. Matthew looked up and the expression on Dirk's face prompted him to say, "Mind if I walk along?"

"Sidewalk's wide enough for two."

Something in Dirk's voice told Matthew that his son-in-law was on guard. "He thinks I'm going to rake him over the coals."

Sunday afternoon was the only time in any week when Oak Hill could be called a sleepy little town. No one was in sight on the street or sidewalks until the two men turned the corner of Walnut and Maple and walked toward the schoolhouse. People were either visiting here or there, eating, or taking naps.

Mary Anne saw them and came down the slide in a running jump and ran to meet them. "Hi, Papa," she said. "You're all dressed up."

"Well it's Sunday," Dirk said.

"Did you come just to see us?"

"I did. I'd have come before but — "

"I know why you didn't," Mary Anne said. "Mama told me. Grandma's been awful sick. Is she better?"

Neal walked up and stood next to Matthew. "Howdy son," Dirk said. "You all right?"

"Yes sir," Neal said.

"Good. I guess you're taking good care of your mother."

"Grandpa's taking care of all of us," Neal said.

Matthew saw a mottled flush rise up to Dirk's ears. *How much pain is he feeling now? Or is it guilt?*

Matthew hurried everyone into the car after Dirk left. He wanted spirits to be bright, not dimmed by talk and thoughts of illness and discord. They drove in the area south of Luray and circled and came back the long way through New Castle. Matthew stopped at a drugstore and bought triple dip ice-cream cones for everyone except the baby. She was fed one scoop

156

from a cardboard dish.

Susan and the children got out at home and Matthew and Nancy went up the street to look at a lot on the other end of town. They'd live in Nancy's house for a while but hoped to build some day.

"Did Susan tell you that Dirk gave her some money?"

"When? When did he have a chance?"

"It was in the letters he gave her. In an envelope without a stamp. Fifty dollars."

"Think she'll keep it? She's determined not to be dependent on the Dirksen money."

"I know. But I think she'll keep it. After I told her she might be robbing Dirk not to, she seemed to change a little."

"*Robbing* him?"

"Of the opportunity to atone. That's maybe what he needs now."

"He looks bad — strained," Matthew said. "In a way I felt as if he was a different man, someone I'd just met. We never did have much of a conversation, come to think of it."

18

Matthew didn't see Dirk or talk to him for three weeks. His son-in-law had stopped by the house one day to leave a smoked ham and a sack of maiden blush apples. Susan spoke briefly of the visit when her father and the children came home from school. "He didn't stay long. Bertha must be much worse. I offered to go see her."

"What did Dirk say to that?"

"That there was no use putting myself through the ordeal. She doesn't recognize anyone."

Nine days later Matthew placed a call to Springvale to give Dirk the news that his second son was four hours old. "I'd have called sooner but figured you'd be asleep."

"No one sleeps much here now," Dirk said. "Is Susan all right? And the little one?"

"I'd say so," Matthew said. "Has the required number of fingers and toes — and strong lungs."

Dirk didn't ask if the baby'd been given a name. Matthew wondered why. Was he too burdened by the ordeal to have a part in naming his son? *A few weeks ago I'd have been sure Dirk would have been angry to hear that Susan has given the baby my name.*

Now — Well — I don't know.

When Little Matt was five weeks old, Matthew took Susan and the older children back to Springvale for Bertha Garland's funeral. Nancy stayed in Oak Hill with the baby.

Dirk and his father sat alone on the front pew in the center section of the Christ's Chapel Church for the first few minutes of the service. Then Mary Anne whispered to her mother and slipped past Matthew's knees, around the end of the seat, and sat between her father and Seth. Dirk darted a backward glance at Susan then put his arm around the little girl and pulled her close.

They were at the cemetery for at least half an hour after the service was over. People wanted to speak to Susan. Matthew took Ellen's hand and went for a walk among what the child called "the big rocks." The feel of fall was in the air. The first frost had been light and the maple trees had lost little of their foliage. They were bouquets of yellow, and blushed in red.

As Matthew led his granddaughter back to the group he wondered what words would be carved on the stone at the head of Bertha's grave. Had she dictated her wishes or would she consider herself immortal? Would she want to be known as a Dirksen in death as she had in life? He shook his head and told himself that such speculation bordered on the morbid. *It's more to the point to wonder what changes will come to Seth and Dirk. Or is this something else that's none of my business?*

Seth Garland came to meet Matthew. "I talked to Susan about this. Do you reckon you could see your way clear to come out to the house for a spell? It might brighten things. Wipe away some of the gloom."

"What did Susan say?"

"That it was up to you."

"Then we'll stop by," Matthew said. He remembered how he'd felt after his mother's funeral. It was a time when he'd realized that a major adjustment was to be made. A time when the world seemed to stop.

Matthew had never been in the big farmhouse. Susan had told him that the heavy oak furniture was dark and that the walls in the kitchen were painted a dull but serviceable gray. Mary Anne took him to the parlor to see the velvet-backed picture made of many kinds of seeds. It was hung so high that he had to stretch to see and Mary Anne asked to be lifted in his arms.

Seth rekindled a fire in the mottled gray kitchen range and Susan measured coffee into the blue granite pot. "Church folks brought in some food," Seth said. "Which is surprising. Seeing none of us took any part. 'Cepting you, Susan. They probably did it for you."

"Maybe not," Susan said. "They have a genuine concern for persons in need."

It was dusk before Susan said, "We'd better go. Nancy's had the baby several hours."

Parting was awkward for all the adults except Seth. He said, "Now you folks come back. And take good care of each other. And the new one."

Matthew looked at Dirk. His face was mirrored pain. He reached into his pocket, put coins in Mary Anne's palm, and folded her fingers around them. "Maybe your Grandpa will take you to the drugstore for some ice cream."

160

"We go by ourselves now, Papa," Mary Anne said. "We're big enough."

"The road between here and Oak Hill runs both ways," Matthew said. "You drop by and see us, Nancy and me."

"And us, Papa," Mary Anne said. "Be sure to bring Grandpa too."

Dirk did visit his family at least once a week for nearly a year. And Susan borrowed her father's car a few times and went out to cook and clean for the two men. Matthew wasn't sure when it became clear that Susan and Dirk would be reconciled. It was like working a complicated problem. One move led to another until the answer came.

Matthew had more trouble analyzing his own feelings. It wasn't a simple matter of addition. He had to subtract his skepticism about the chances that a man's nature would change. His feelings were divided between protectiveness for Susan and fairness toward Dirk — and every other man.

He didn't question Susan but he quizzed Nancy whenever he thought she'd had a chance to find out how his daughter felt. One evening he asked, "How do you think the land lies? Is there a sound basis for a reconciliation?"

"Matthew Kirk! You never cease to amaze me."

"How can a man answer a remark like that? What have I done to engender a state of amazement? To set you on your tin ear?"

"There you go again. In one sentence you sound so profound. Like a teacher. Then you use common sayings in the next breath."

"Do I do that?"

"You do."

"I wonder why?" Matthew said.

"That's easy to understand," Nancy said. "It's part of that overall view of yours. The way you see life. From more than one side at once."

"That doesn't seem strange to me. There *are* many sides to everyone and to all situations. But you got me off the track. Do you see any indication that Susan's going to move back to Springvale?"

Eight days later Matthew's question was answered — not by Nancy nor Susan, but by Dirk. Nancy was at church when the old pickup truck came down the cinder alley behind the house. Matthew had sprained his foot the day before as he spaded willow sprouts from the lot on which he and Nancy planned to build. His foot had slipped and he'd slid down the bank, landing in a twisted position. He was limping out to the trash burner when he saw Dirk.

"Morning, sir. What happened to you?"

"I suppose you could say I threw my weight around — in the wrong way."

"That's hard to believe," Dirk said. "You never do that — never butt in."

Matthew knew that his son-in-law had come for a purpose. "Want to go inside?" he asked.

"It's all right out here. When the sun hits us. Pa calls this real Indian summer weather."

"Then pull a chair over to the east side. We'll be out of the wind."

"Susan wanted to come," Dirk said as he drummed his fingers on the wide arm of the lawn chair. "But

I figured it was up to me to break this ground."

"You're going back together?"

Dirk looked straight at Matthew. Then he smiled.
Did I ever see him do that? Matthew thought, *I don't remember.*

"Yes, we are," Dirk said. "It's been a long time coming. And most of the time I thought this day would never get here. It seemed too good, too much to hope for."

"Then Susan will be moving back to Springvale?"

"No. No. I wouldn't ask that of her. Or do that to the kids. The house where we lived is more rundown. And Ma's house could never be Susan's home. Besides, the kids like this school. And this town."

Matthew asked Dirk if he thought he'd get tired of driving back and forth every day.

"Could be," Dirk said. "But there are worse things for a man."

"You moving in now — today?"

"No. Probably not. I'm taking Susan and the children out to the farm to talk about the whole thing. And that's partly why I'm here. We'd like for you and Mrs. Kirk to come."

"Sounds funny to hear you call Nancy Mrs. Kirk."

"Well, I don't know her very well."

"I guess that's right. But going back. Why do you want us in on this? Is this Susan's idea?"

"Partly. The whole idea is that it's sort of a family confab. We think the kids will feel better. We think you can help."

"Then I'm fairly sure we'll come. Nancy will be home in about a half an hour. Say — if we don't go,

163

how are you going to haul all your family in the truck?"

"No problem," Dirk said. "Pa drove the car in. We're leaving it for Susan."

By evening a few of the frayed places in the Kirk-Garland family relationship were mended. Susan and Nancy pooled what they'd prepared for Sunday dinner and they all sat down at the Garland's rectangular oak table in the long dining room. The dark green window shades were rolled past the halfway mark.

Seth looked around as he passed the meat loaf to Dirk. "I don't know as we ever did eat in here. Or did we?"

"Not that I remember," Dirk said. "In fact I doubt that these extra table boards have ever been used."

Evidently Susan had told the children that their father would be living with them. So when she brought up the subject at the table there were no awkward pauses except for the fact that Neal made no comment. Matthew watched the boy's face. *He keeps looking at Susan. He's wondering if she's happy or sad.*

Mary Anne, as usual, was vocal. "What are you going to do, Grandpa Garland? Are you going to live with us too?"

"That wouldn't be a bad idea," Seth said. "From my point of view. But I figure I'm needed here. To watch over things."

"But this big house," Nancy said. "Isn't it lonely?"

"It always was," Seth said. "And I got an egg of an idea about that. It's not ready for hatching."

"Are you going home with us, Papa?" Mary Anne

164

asked as they walked out to the car.

"No. Not for a day or two. This old truck is about past going. We're going to see about trading it in tomorrow. So I can make it back and forth."

"Could you and Nancy come back after the children's bedtime?" Susan asked before she climbed out of the car. "I want to tell you what helped me come to a decision."

"Well. We can," Matthew said. "But this is your business."

"I know. But I want *you* to know."

It was nearly nine o'clock before Nancy came home from evening services. She didn't want to go but had promised to play the organ. "Should we drive?" she asked, "on account of your foot?"

"I can hobble along. If you're not ashamed to be seen with me wearing one felt house slipper."

"Well, it's dark, and if we meet anyone I can walk ahead and pretend I don't know you," Nancy said. "So come on."

Susan was alone and waiting and came right to the point. "This has been a soul-searching time," she said. "Not only for me. Dirk's had to do some serious thinking and fact facing."

She told them that Bertha Garland's will had altered Dirk's thinking. "She left Seth out — except for a small share of the income. And this both shocked and changed Dirk. He said that he might have seen things in a different light a year ago. That having us leave and realizing how you took care of us, gave him a new idea of family."

"A new idea?" Nancy said.

"Yes. Not just people of the same name handing on land and money. He'd never thought of it as meaning a loving unit."

"That's sad," Nancy said.

"Is that what inclined you toward going back? Or having him come here?"

"It inclined me, yes," Susan said. "That wasn't the deciding factor, but it did prove that he'd changed. That his mother's grip was broken."

She leaned her head back on the high back of her mother's rocker. "I suppose the clincher came when Dirk said I should go back and finish college. That was an about-face. His mother had drilled the idea into him that woman's role didn't take book learning. Her last illness must have revealed a lot to Dirk. But he doesn't say much about it. Probably never will.

"I want this to work, Papa," Susan said. "I want the children not only to have two parents — but two who care. Do you think I'm wrong?" She looked at Nancy then at Matthew.

"I told your father some time ago that I hoped you wouldn't rob Dirk of the opportunity to atone," Nancy said.

The room was still for a few minutes except for the ticking of the clock and the creak of a loose rocker. "You know, Nancy," Susan said. "You've put my feelings into words. That is what I'm doing. How about you, Papa?"

"Honey, I trust your instincts. I always have."

19

A renewed sense of balance came into Matthew's thinking after Dirk came to Oak Hill to live. "I never thought of Susan and the children as a burden," he told Nancy late one winter afternoon. "But I did feel responsible. In fact I have from the time she was married."

"Some people never shed that responsibility," Nancy said. "Don't even want to in some cases."

"What do you mean?"

"Oh Matt! You surely have seen cases where either mothers or fathers want to think of themselves as either matriarchs or patriarchs — in a domineering sense, I mean."

"I've run on to a few," Matthew said. He walked to the front window and stood for a minute. They'd moved into the new brick house at Thanksgiving and he hadn't quite oriented himself to his surroundings. The picture of the new setting wasn't in focus. The houses and trees and even the horizon looked different from this end of the street. He was on higher ground, a new vantage point.

"I can see the back chimney on the Crandall house," he said. "I don't remember noticing that before.

And I can see a wider stretch of State Route 3 from here."

"You've always seen more than anyone else," Nancy said. "Aren't you ever going to be satisfied with the near view?"

"Probably not. Not as long as there's a horizon and that's unlimited."

"But you don't seem to want to travel to faraway places."

"I know why," Matthew said. "I'm afraid I'd be disappointed. I've read about Philadelphia and Mt. Vernon and London and such places. I have them pictured in my mind. And I'm not sure the reality would be as satisfying. So I might be wasting my money and time."

The sun seemed to linger longer than on other December evenings. It left traces of rose and gold above the lacy black of the tree-rimmed horizon. Nancy had put oyster stew on to simmer and was grading papers while the peppered soup heated. Matthew walked from one window to another.

"Are you restless for some reason?" Nancy asked.

"No. Not exactly. But I crossed a line today. Not an international dateline. But a kind of Kirk milestone. I began to think ahead to retirement."

"Don't you feel well?"

"I feel fine. Otherwise I wouldn't be looking ahead. I'd be pulling back."

Nancy took off her gold-rimmed eyeglasses and put the sheaf of papers in a woven straw handbag. "Come on to the kitchen. Tell me while we eat."

The kitchen was on the east side and Matthew took

a glance in that direction and to the south before he sat down. He lingered longer at the back window.

"What do you see out there that you've never noticed before?"

"This time I'm seeing something that isn't there. I think I'll build a garage on the rise of ground, instead of in the side yard."

"For any particular reason?" Nancy asked as she ladled steaming stew into blue willowware bowls. "Now why did I put it that way? You always have a reason."

"Because it's there. And high. And dry. Besides, that bank will be hard to mow. A building will use up a little of the space."

He talked of possible shapes and materials. "I like brick and this house suits me fine. But I like to work with wood and now's the time to sharpen my skill — if any."

Nancy asked how building a garage tied in with the idea of retirement. She said this project wouldn't last him very long.

"It's a step," Matthew said. He hadn't told Nancy or anyone of the idea he'd had in his mind since he first moved to Oak Hill. It came one day when he moved the oxen yokes and other relics from the shed in Richmond to the small barn on Maple Street. He knew that the purchases he'd made at auction sales were considered as a waste of money to many people. *But today's junk will be tomorrow's antiques,* he often thought.

Matthew never intended to sell the tools and trappings of other days for a profit. He wanted to start a museum. There wasn't another one in Delaware

County, and as far as he knew no one was considering the idea. *Maybe some folks'd say it ought to be in the county seat. But I don't live in Muncie.*

Nancy broke into his thinking by asking if he wanted raspberry pie or canned applesause for dessert. "Where were you?" she asked. "I've put this question to you twice."

"I was somewhere in the future. Taking some other steps in my mind."

"And you're not ready to talk about them yet. Right?"

"Well, ideas are fragile until you put them into practice. Talking about them before they're fully formed — I guess it's a kind of abortion."

"Won't you miss teaching — miss seeing the students?"

"I couldn't miss seeing them — at least the former ones. I meet them on the street every day. Except those who've moved away. Or didn't come back from the war."

Matthew did a lot of thinking about the futility of war. As a history teacher he couldn't agree that bloodshed was the way to settle differences between nations. As far as he was concerned battlefield deaths were a type of murder. He often wondered if his years at a Quaker college had influenced his thinking. He always concluded that he'd never liked to fight, hadn't even gone hunting, and even felt guilty the three times he'd caught a silver-scaled fish. Such meditations led him to wonder what he'd have done if he'd been within draft age. *I'd have been a conscientious objector but would I have said so? Would draft boards give exemptions to people who didn't belong to denominations*

170

that traditionally oppose war? This was one of the things Matthew hadn't learned, either from books or from experience.

Matthew had three years to step into retirement. He did a little prospecting into the future by working part time at the lumberyard. They hired him after he'd wandered up and down between piles of stacked boards several times, before buying materials for his garage. "They told me they could use anyone who asked so many questions," Matthew told his wife.

"I don't understand *that*," Nancy said.

"The way the owner put it was that a person had to have real interest and some knowledge in order to ask good questions."

"I guess that's right," Nancy said. "Making out tests is not the easiest part of teaching."

Seth Garland had given Matthew the opportunity to serve an apprenticeship in woodworking. He'd revealed his plan to move out of the big farmhouse about the time Dirk moved into Oak Hill. He converted the little barn on a knoll beyond the yard into a cozy home. The two grandfathers enjoyed working on the project and the whole family followed their progress. Susan and Nancy made curtains and chose pans and dishes for Seth's small kitchen. The lighting of the first flame in the wide fireplace was a cause for celebration. Its light and its warmth were symbols of a new era in the Garland family. The shadowy influence of the Dirksens was being dispersed.

By the time Little Matt was five years old, not only the garage but the addition of a wide veranda sat on the back of the lot. Matthew didn't intend to rock his life away. But he liked to survey the scene now and then. He'd stop on the way home from the lumberyard, rock awhile, and look around Oak Hill. Or he'd play dominoes with Neal on Sunday afternoon and catch up on what was in the boy's wondering mind, and what was happening at school.

Neal was a good reporter. Sometimes Matthew thought the boy made a point of looking in all the rooms so he'd have something to tell his grandfather. "The first-grade teacher has a big plant in her room. But she must be doing something wrong. It has a bunch of yellow leaves."

Now on this Memorial Day Matthew sat on the veranda and looked out over the town and on life as it was now. The view was pleasing to his mind. Susan and Dirk had rebuilt their relationship. It couldn't have been easy for either. Susan surely had remembered the years she hurt and Dirk must have had difficulty forgetting that he'd caused much of her unhappiness.

Dirk had been uncomfortable with Susan's family for several months and Matthew could see that his son-in-law still didn't feel at home in Oak Hill. He rarely went to the general store and never to church. Matthew wondered, *Do wisps of Bertha's antagonism toward church still cling in his mind? Or can't he face an aggregate of people who may know why Susan left him?*

Matthew pulled his gold watch out of his vest pocket. *Only nine-thirty. Time hangs heavy when I'm idle. Maybe that's the best part of holidays. They give us a chance to appreciate having work to do.* He got up, walked to the corner of the porch, and looked up

172

at the sky. *Not a cloud in sight. That means we can eat out here. I'll set up the trestle tables before Susan and the children get here.* He wasn't sure why he was glad for fair weather. *Is it because indoor picnics aren't fun for the children? Or because I keep wanting to justify myself for building this veranda?*

A kaleidoscope of bright thoughts formed a pattern in his mind. Susan was back in school. Neal didn't seem to be afraid of his father, and Dirk had a good relationship with Seth. Words from a poem stood out in his consciousness.

"God's in His heaven and all's right with the world."

Maybe that's not exactly true, Matthew thought as he sat down in the twine-seated rocker. *There are troubled people all over this world. Even right here in Oak Hill. But at this moment, from where I sit, life looks good.*

THE AUTHOR

Dorothy Hamilton has lived in Delaware County, Indiana, all her life. She attended school at Cowan, Muncie Central High, and Ball State University. She has been active in professional writing courses, first as a student and later as an instructor.

Mrs. Hamilton grew up in the Methodist Church and devoted much of her life to rearing seven children.

Then she felt led to become a private tutor. Several hundred girls and boys have come to Mrs. Hamilton for gentle encouragement, for renewal of their self-esteem, and to improve their schoolwork.

Since 1967 she has had fifty serials, more than fifty short stories, and several articles published in religious magazines. She has also written for radio and newspaper.

Mrs. Hamilton is author of a growing shelf of books: *Anita's Choice, Christmas for Holly, Charco, The Killdeer, Tony Savala, Jim Musco, Settled Furrows, Kerry, The Blue Caboose, Mindy, The Quail, The Gift of a Home, Jason,* and *Busboys at Big Bend.*